A FASCINATING REPORT ON THE AMAZING MR. JAMES BOND

BACKGROUND:	Swiss mother, Scottish father; public school education; sent down from Eton
DESCRIPTION:	Tall, dark, tiger-muscled; scar down right side of face; thin, cruel mouth
WEAPONS:	.25 Beretta automatic in left arm holster; knife; judo
WOMEN:	Duchesses, doxies, crooks, countesses. Married briefly to Tracy, la Comtesse di Vicenzo
OCCUPATION:	Paid professional killer in the service of British espionage
COMMENT:	DANGEROUS

Now, in addition to the SMERSH files in Moscow and M's dossier in Regent's Park, comes this new report on Agent 007: his image, his adversaries, his women. It's a book that lays bare the mind and soul of the intrepid secret agent and it's as spellbinding as any of Bond's own extravagant adventures.

SIGNET Adventure Novels by Ian Fleming
Featuring James Bond

50¢ each

CASINO ROYALE	(#D1997)
DIAMONDS ARE FOREVER	(#D2029)
DOCTOR NO	(#D2036)
FOR YOUR EYES ONLY	(#D2054)
FROM RUSSIA, WITH LOVE	(#D2030)
GOLDFINGER	(#D2052)
LIVE AND LET DIE	(#D2051)
MOONRAKER	(#D2053)
ON HER MAJESTY'S SECRET SERVICE	(#D2509)
THE SPY WHO LOVED ME	(#D2280)
THUNDERBALL	(#D2126)

TO OUR READERS: If your dealer does not have the SIGNET and MENTOR books you want, you may order them by mail, enclosing the list price plus 10¢ a copy to cover mailing. If you would like our free catalog, please request it by postcard. The New American Library of World Literature, Inc., P. O. Box 2310, Grand Central Station, New York, N. Y. 10017.

007
JAMES BOND:
A
Report

by O. F. SNELLING

A SIGNET BOOK
Published by THE NEW AMERICAN LIBRARY

© O. F. Snelling, London 1964

All rights reserved

First Printing, April, 1965

A hardcover edition of this title is published
in England by Neville Spearman—The Holland Press.

SIGNET TRADEMARK REG. U.S. PAT. OFF. AND FOREIGN COUNTRIES
REGISTERED TRADEMARK—MARCA REGISTRADA
HECHO EN CHICAGO, U.S.A.

SIGNET BOOKS are published by
The New American Library of World Literature, Inc.
501 Madison Avenue, New York, New York 10022

PRINTED IN THE UNITED STATES OF AMERICA

To
RICHARD USBORNE
'onlie begetter'
How's *that* for originality?

Contents

His Predecessors   11

His Image   16

His Women   35

His Adversaries   86

His Future   118

Acknowledgments

DURING THE WRITING of this book many friends and acquaintances had all sorts of ideas and suggestions the minute they knew what I was up to. Much that was offered could be used: just as much didn't quite fit in with what I was trying to do but was nevertheless equally useful in its way. It gave me an idea of people's reactions. To all those who expressed interest and opinions when I confided my folly I am extremely grateful.

A few others, who, either from direct request or out of sheer love of me and enthusiasm for the idea of what I was doing brought to my attention certain facts, reviews, reports and essays which I am sure I would otherwise have missed, I take pleasure in naming. They are Neville Armstrong, A. A. Bellhouse, Melba Kershaw, Edward Lazare, Gerald Leach, Peter Noble, Martin Orskey, Joan Potter, Alex Rogoyski, Molly Sudéal, Julian Stedman and Brenda and Gladstone Williams.

I should also like to say thank you to the Kingston, Jamaica, *Daily Gleaner*, prolific in its coverage of both James Bond and Ian Fleming, to John Hall of *Encounter*, for information he very obligingly gave me, to Thomas Tait & Sons, Ltd., for permission to use their watermark, to Ian Fleming himself for writing the books I have enjoyed so much and to Jonathan Cape Ltd. for publishing them.

I offer an equally brief sentiment, quite unprintable, to the staff of a publication who did not even deign to answer my letters, presumably because there was nothing in it for them, apart from a mere acknowledgment here, if they did.

Author's Note

AFTER THIS BOOK had been written and had gone to press, Ian Fleming's new James Bond book, *You Only Live Twice,* was published. In it there appears a somewhat premature obituary notice of the Secret Service agent. This ill-timed obituary serves a particular purpose: it supplies the answer to quite a few of the queries posed in the following pages. From it, for example, we learn that Bond was at Eton, which we had suspected anyway. We also learn a bit about his upbringing. It also transpires that he's had a sort of Dr. Watson, all these years, writing 'high-flown and romanticized caricatures of episodes in the career of an outstanding public servant.' I think it a coincidence worth mentioning that the actor who portrayed Sherlock Holmes' famous colleague and confidant in many well-remembered pre-war films should bear the same name as this latter-day Dr. Watson.

The obituary, unfortunately, doesn't clear up everything. As far as Bond's early chronology is concerned, I find things in greater confusion than ever.

I would have liked to have dealt with *You Only Live Twice* in this book. But short of re-writing every chapter this was impossible. But I have added one or two footnotes wherever I felt the matter was relevant.

And, although I can't write about them, I take this opportunity of welcoming Tiger Tanaka and Kissy Suzuki among my more pleasant acquaintances.

His Predecessors

IN 1953 TWO remarkable books were published. One was *Casino Royale*, a first novel by Ian Fleming—but more of that later. The other was a fascinating and extremely readable little volume entitled *Clubland Heroes*. Nothing quite like it had ever been done before. Its author, Richard Usborne, set out to examine certain of the writings and characters of three popular authors of his youth: John Buchan, Sapper and Dornford Yates.

It is significant that each of these best-sellers produced the bulk of his work in an era that was pre-1939, and it is no coincidence that they all dealt with characters who might collectively be termed Upper Class. In the 1960s—and, indeed, when Usborne wrote about them—they appeared more than a little archaic.

Richard Usborne delightfully analyses a great deal of the writings of his three authors loosely coming under the heading of 'thrillers' or 'light' fiction. As he points out, Buchan wrote fifty-seven books, but less than twenty are dealt with; Sapper wrote a number of stories which were of a quite different nature from the ones for which he will be remembered; on the other hand, almost everything of Yates' is touched upon, because practically all of it comes within the province of Usborne's book.

Ten main characters are placed under the microscope. With the exception of Carl Peterson, Sapper's arch-criminal and one of the most infamous villains of sensational fiction, all are cast in the same mould. They are all West End clubmen, they all appear to be of independent means and they all conform to a rigid code of honour made up by equal parts of birth, public school, university and the army. They are all extremely masculine, virile and, paradoxically, utterly emasculated.

Of the ten characters examined, only three need concern us here. John Buchan will forever be associated with Richard Hannay; Sapper's foremost hero is, of course, Bulldog Drummond, and Dornford Yates' protagonist in this particular *genre* is undoubtedly Jonah Mansel. Hannay, Drummond and Mansel: the Terrible Trio of popular fiction between the two wars. Millions of readers have thrilled to the exploits of these imaginary but none the less very real adventurers. But how do they stand up today beside Ian Fleming's sophisticated and sardonic Secret Service agent, Commander James Bond?

It is not my intention to elaborate *too* greatly on the Clubland Heroes of Richard Usborne's. Mention of his book, and its contents, is here used as a stepping-off point towards an examination of a writer and his fictional character, neither of whom we might ever have heard but for the sterling spade-work done in earlier years by John Buchan, Sapper and Dornford Yates.

But certain comparisons need to be drawn. James Bond, like the Terrible Trio, is of the clubland stratum of society, if he is not exactly a hero. He is comfortably off, and always has been, even if he does do a job of work too. He moves easily in places like the Ritz, the Hotel de Paris, and the sporting clubs and private rooms of continental casinos. He understands the code of people like Hannay, Drummond and Mansel, upheld to a large extent by M, his chief, who holds 'a great deal of his affection and all his loyalty', but he does not live by it. Had he been born twenty to thirty years earlier he might have been very much like one of the Trio himself—rather like Sapper's Ronald Standish, perhaps. The generation that separates Bond from the Clubland Heroes has made all the difference. The code of honour and the morality that bred Buchan and his contemporaries in late Victorian days did not obtain during the Edwardian and Georgian era that produced Ian Fleming.

Hannay was a country gentleman, a man who understood the Scottish crofter and thought him the salt of the earth, but he was always The Squire. Drummond, a West End man-about-town, could mix with the common herd when occasion demanded it, and could even disguise himself and pass himself off as a member of the working class, but in his mind the masses were always The Great Unwashed. Mansel, and more particularly Dornford Yates, who sired him, who was totally incapable of not colouring all his heroes with his own personality and predilections, was a downright snob. Yates was a Colonel Blimp so Blimpish that he was utterly unaware that he was practically a caricature.

James Bond is a latter-day member of their Set who has Gone Off the Rails, a renegade Etonian type who has been mixing with the Townies. He will always be accepted in their clubs, because he knows The Form. They, of course, can flirt with an Irma Peterson or play up to a Vanity Fair just as well as he can, in the line of duty, but they would die a thousand deaths rather than not Do the Decent Thing. They would never soil their clean-limbed bodies by any intimacy with such sluts. They don't stop at the bedroom door: they never get that far. Bond, on the other hand, recognizes and honours no code in this direction. He doesn't care if the girl of the moment is a duchess or a doxy, a crook or a countess. As long as she is personable, that will do. As for bedrooms, and bedroom doors, they might just as well not exist. Bubble cars, beach huts, liner cabins, train compartments or secluded glades—they're all the same to him, as long as there is a modicum of privacy.

Bond lives in an age of jet planes, which carry him to New York in a few hours and to the Caribbean in a few hours more. The inhabitants of the western hemisphere are as familiar to him as were Hampshire men to Mansel and Highlanders to Hannay. Americans are not the gum-chewing extroverts in horn-rimmed spectacles, improbable creatures from some far-off zoo that they appeared to be, almost to a man, in the view of at least two of the Terrible Trio back in the 1920s. They are people like Felix Leiter. There are *some* larger than life American characters in Fleming's world, with picturesque names and even more picturesque speech, but no unlikely stereotypes christened Franklin P. Scudder (Buchan), Hiram K. Potts (Sapper) or Coker Falk (Yates).

It could be argued, of course, that I have snatched at the convenience of Usborne's Clubland Heroes, and that they have little in common—even by comparison—with James Bond. I admit that he would probably be far more comfortable in the company of, say, Leslie Charteris' Simon Templar, the Saint, from the little I know of that character. I know little of him because he seems to me a mere ghost, or at the most a lay figure jouncing and swashbuckling through an interminable number of books and stories which are forgotten almost as soon as they are read. Sensational fiction is full of slightly caddish protagonists, non-heroes who appear to be—on the face of things—closer to Bond than the illustrious triumvirate. These range from the gentleman-cracksman type like the early Raffles and the later Blackshirt to the tough, cynical Private Eye like Philip Marlowe and the hooligans of Mickey Spillane. It *could* be argued that Bond has more in common with any of these than with Hannay, Drummond and Mansel.

Personally, I don't think he has. The Terrible Trio were *alive*. We can believe in them as real people, despite the outrageous adventures they all got up to. Their authors drew their portraits, their characters and their backgrounds. But what do we really know of Philip Marlowe, for example? I have read all of the Raymond Chandler books but I can recall Marlowe only as a vague operator in a rather sleazy office working on the Pacific coast in towns with Spanish-sounding names. This may be because, firstly, Chandler wrote who-dun-its, and was primarily concerned with his plots and not with his people, and secondly, because the fictional Marlowe relates the stories himself, and the opportunity for characterization is limited. Yet the Richard Hannay books of John Buchan's are all written in the first person, too. But I find that I can remember more of *The Three Hostages*, for example, than of the whole of Chandler's output.

It is just possible that Richard Usborne has vitalized his Clubland Heroes in one minor masterpiece in a manner their creators never achieved in book after book. Perhaps if Usborne, or someone else, were to take characters like the Saint, Marlowe or Inspector Maigret* they could become as real to me as the Trio? I doubt it: I don't think the material is there to start with.

I believe that Usborne did for his particular heroes what many writers have also done for Sherlock Holmes. Conan Doyle did it first in his stories, and he did it so well that Holmes and Watson became household names and living people to many thousands in the 1890s. To a lesser extent Buchan, Sapper and Yates brought their characters to life while Usborne was still a boy who read about them and had no idea of writing about them. Ian Fleming is doing the same thing today, with James Bond, better than any of them.

He is doing it better because he is giving his readers exactly what they want. The three of his predecessors I am concerned with here gave their public what they thought was good for them. Buchan, Sapper and Dornford Yates were English gentlemen—well, British gentlemen, anyway—staunch conservative 'literary blokes' who believed wholeheartedly in what they were doing: Upholding the Code, Carrying the Flag, Maintaining the Breed. Their attitude has since been referred to, more than once, as 'fascist'. I imagine they might have been proud of this, rather than otherwise. Fleming has also been awarded the same designation, on occasion, but unjustifiably, in my opinion. I doubt if he gives a damn.

The Terrible Trio were fictional characters, and yet they weren't all *that* fictional. Each was based on someone their

* A friend of mine, who has been reading, and enjoying Simenon's works for many years, confesses that he is often more than halfway through a story before it occurs to him that he has read it before. I doubt if this could happen with a Bond book.

authors knew and admired. Over the years, if these characters developed and took on more and more of their creators' own personalities as the time passed, well, so much the better. No harm in a dig or two against The Enemy, whether he be the Bolshevik Bogey of the 'twenties or the Welfare State of the 'forties. Same thing, really. Ian Fleming, I feel, would never deny that there is a great deal of himself in James Bond, and yet his aproach is very different from that of the others. SMERSH and Soviet Russia were expedient villains when the Cold War was frosty; recent years have found him less inclined to blame the world's ills on the Kremlin. I can never imagine Dornford Yates, though, attempting to shift the responsibility elsewhere. I am sure that in his opinion even a liberal-minded Tory was financed by Moscow Gold. Fleming, wherever he may put his cross at the polling-booth—and we can't be as certain about this as we can be about the others—has no particular message in his books, in my submission: no axe to grind beyond that of giving his readers a good yarn that they can accept and believe.

Few critics have successfully analysed the best seller. But one who did, I think, was Q. D. Leavis. In her *Fiction and the Reading Public* I believe that she made it apparent that best-sellerdom and complete sincerity were synonymous. To top the charts, as they say today, you had to believe that you were a gift from God, like Marie Corelli or Hall Caine, writing deathless prose. Rather more sensationally, Buchan, Sapper and Dornford Yates, in company with contemporaries like P. C. Wren, fall into this category.

Ian Fleming, I suggest, is an exception. He may not have hit precisely upon the infallible recipe for producing highly-successful novels—the formula that so many serious students of literature have been seeking for so long, and have been failing to find—but he knows most of the ingredients. In 1961 his publishers told us that two million copies of his books had been sold in English alone, and that figure has considerably increased since then. The extremely enjoyable films of the books have now earned James Bond many thousands of new devotees: people who never read reviews, literary magazines or, in some cases, even newspapers, and who had blithely lived through the past few years in a fools' paradise, unaware that fiction now had the 'livingest' character since Sherlock Holmes. Many of these enlightened film-goers, high upon a peak in Darien, now avidly read every one of the books they could find. Finding them wasn't hard: most of them had been readily available in moderately-priced paperback editions for years, if they had only looked. Now it became almost impossible not to notice them. I should think that every self-respecting bookstall in the country has them on view.

The snowball grows. Not everyone, of course, exactly *likes* James Bond, but few people can resist the temptation to talk about him and pass a lengthy opinion on him. The blurb of the Cape edition of *Thunderball* says:

> ... Bond has been described as 'the most controversial thriller hero of the century'. To his fans he is a tough undercover commando who serves his country and gets hurt (and girls!) in the process. His critics mutter 'sex, sadism and snobbery'. Fleming, unperturbed, says, 'Bond is not a hero, nor is he depicted as being very likeable or admirable. He is a Secret Service agent. He's not a bad man, but he is ruthless and self-indulgent. He enjoys the fight—he also enjoys the prizes. In fiction, people used to have blood in their veins. Nowdays they have pond water. My books are just out of step. But then so are all the people who read them.'

Before long, the way things are going, everyone in the army will be out of step except the few people who *don't* read them.

In this book, by somewhat impertinently dissecting Bond in the *Clubland Heroes* manner, I hope it will not be construed that I am anti-Fleming. The fact is that he has no greater admirer than myself.

I am not trying to emulate Richard Usborne. As one of his subjects would say, 'that were impossible'. But I do admit to trying to imitate him. In his introduction, he refers to 'characters whom I have, for thirty years, happily regarded as real people,' and he goes on to say that he often strays into 'examining them, rather unfairly, *as* real people.' I do the same thing in the following pages. He calls his approach the Lower Criticism. If my examination is criticism at all, it might be termed, perhaps, the Lowest Criticism.

His Image

WHEN WE FIRST heard of him he was Commander James Bond, R.N.V.R. He is now entitled to append the initials C.M.G., but he probably never will.

His Image

He has worked for the British Secret Service since about 1938 or 1939.* He is now no. 007, 'the senior of the three men in the Service who had earned the double 0 number', which licenses him to kill.

So far, we know very little about his early life or even about his war-time experiences, but we do know that he has been dicing with death on behalf of his country for quite ten or eleven years, and probably more. His exploits have been faithfully chronicled over this period and he is a very valuable man to Her Majesty's Government. He is an equally valuable man to have about if anyone on his side is in a tight spot.

Bond's age is indeterminate. In *Moonraker* (1955), he was in his middle thirties. Therefore, in 1945, at the end of the war, he must have been in his middle twenties—let's say twenty-six. We know that he has worked for the Secret Service since *before* the war, so he would have been in his late 'teens when he first began this exacting and exciting work. He is a former naval man: a fact betrayed by the letters behind his name as well as the prefix of Commander. Just what and who he commanded we are not told, but if it was during the war, as it probably was, he must have been fairly youthful to hold such a responsible position. In *Thunderball* (1961), when, presumably, he was in his early forties, the violent, nervewracking life he leads does not appear to have aged him. Domino Vitali, a perceptive cutie, looks him up and down, notes everything from the 'dark, rather cruel good looks and very clear blue-grey eyes' to the inevitable 'black knitted silk tie' and assumes that he is 'somewhere in his middle thirties.'

We lesser mortals, envious of, but not jealous of Bond's attributes, are rather piqued at this. Why doesn't *he* grow older, as the rest of us do? But then perhaps this particular adventure is not being narrated in strict chronological sequence? Like a Baker Street Irregular, searching line after line of the Sherlock Holmes stories to establish the exact location of no. 221B, the reader scans the tale. Initially, perhaps, it is done in the hope that no evidence will come to light that James is, indeed, approaching middle age.

But don't we soon dissect this story with the growing expectation that evidence *will* be found that Bond is mortal, like us? I did, for one. But is the feeling disappointment, or smug satisfaction that is experienced when Bond turns to

---

* According to 'Obit:', Chapter 21 of *You Only Live Twice*, he was in his early 'teens at the time, and still at school. He probably helped his country out during the Long Vac.

Felix Leiter and refers to 'that Moonraker incident of a *few years ago*'? The italics, of course, are not Ian Fleming's.

In a short story called 'For Your Eyes Only', published in 1960 in a book with the same title, M, Bond's chief, says that very few people keep tough after about forty. 'They've been knocked about by life—had troubles, tragedies, illnesses. These things soften you up... How's your coefficient of toughness, James? You haven't got to the dangerous age yet.'

Now since this remark appears in a book of more or less unrelated stories and not in one describing a full-length Bond adventure, it is reasonable to assume that these 'Five Secret Occasions in the Life of James Bond'—the sub-title of the book—didn't all happen one after the other. They probably occurred at various intervals during his career between the bigger occasions. Perhaps Bond *was* in his middle thirties then. But let us hope that he doesn't mark time for ever at that flattering age, like the fading deb who is perennially twenty-nine, or like Billy Bunter and the boys at Greyfriars, who never grew up over several generations.

James Bond's mother was Swiss.* His father was Scottish: a Highlander from near Glencoe. Neither Bond nor his creator lets drop much more about his family background. But he is certainly an educated man, he was presumably at both public school and university, and he was obviously born into the comfortably-off upper middle class.

He has 'a thousand a year free of tax of his own.' In 1955, at the time of the Moonraker adventure, his salary was £1,500 a year. His net income, after tax was deducted, was £2,000 a year. When he is on a job he does not, naturally, use his own money, but during the idle months he does. Since he feels that he will eventually be killed in the line of duty, and since he appears to have no relatives and few dependants, he is determined to have the smallest amount possible in his bank account when his time comes. He therefore spends practically the whole of his income. As most of the people who read about him are wage-earners, they would think of his rate of expenditure as being about £40 a week. In 1955 we were told that 'he could live very well' on this. Those reading about him can well believe it.

His home is a small, comfortable flat in Chelsea, in a plane-tree lined square off the King's Road. Which particular square is not positively identified, but we can place the spot within two or three hundred yards. Richard Usborne admit-

* 'Bond is Scottish. On both sides, as I shall explain in my next book.' Ian Fleming to John Cruesemann, in an interview in the *Daily Express*, 2 January 1964.

ted that even now he could never walk past places like Half Moon Street without imagining himself to be Bulldog Drummond: well, I don't go quite as far as that, but I never walk along King's Road, Chelsea, without glancing into each of those very pleasant squares without wondering which anonymous-looking house shelters James Bond.

He lives alone, with the exception of an elderly housekeeper named May, a Scottish treasure who is obviously devoted to him but who maintains an attitude of polite disapproval towards her employer. She knows that his work is of a dangerous and somewhat secretive nature and she must suffer agonies of curiosity to learn more about it, but she is far too independent to make efforts to find out. Over the years she has changed a little: in *From Russia, With Love* (1957), we are introduced to her thus:

> 'Good morning-s.' (To Bond, one of May's endearing qualities was that she would call no man 'sir' except—Bond had teased her about it years before—English kings and Winston Churchill. As a mark of exceptional regard, she accorded Bond an occasional hint of an 's' at the end of a word.)

By *Thunderball* (1961), she has dropped this habit and refers to him constantly as 'Mister James'. Her accent has also grown perceptibly far more Scottish than it used to be.

Since the flat is a small one and May, presumably, is never very far away, Bond seldom brings his women home. Most of his wenching is done elsewhere.

Tiffany Case was an exception. Bond had an uncomfortable minute or two trying to explain the position on the telephone to M towards the end of *Diamonds are Forever*. 'I'm putting her up in my flat. In the spare room, that is. Very good housekeeper. She'll look after her until I get back. I'm sure she'll be all right, Sir.' He sweated profusely during this conversation. He probably sweated a lot more when he did get back and the assignment was over. Between books— and *how* I wish we knew what happened in the interim— what with Tiffany and May in the same small flat Bond's life must have been like an extended bedroom farce.

When he is not on a job, Bond's office hours are from about ten to six. He spends them, mostly, at a desk in a rather mysterious building near Regent's Park. Ostensibly, he works for a firm called Universal Export, the managing director of which is a fascinating bloke known as M. By now, I should imagine, this cover is pretty well blown. Every undercover organization on earth must know that it's really the headquarters of the British Secret Service and that M is the cove who bosses the gaff. The Union Corse has tumbled, for a start, and SPECTRE has tabs, too. I can't see Universal Export lasting much longer.

Be that as it may, it's where James Bond works, putting in his daily stint of reading inter-office memos, a dull existence relieved by practice with firearms or unarmed combat, further lightened by the occasional pleasant lunch or a mild flirtation. Without these diversions I am sure he would very soon go up the pole. He is a man of action: dangerous living is the breath of life to him. Routine office-work bores him stiff. Fortuitously, M can usually be relied upon to buzz him, and the old red light of privacy will always go on when Bond is at his lowest ebb.

His leisure seems to be passed at fast driving, playing cards—at both of which he is an expert, by the way—or in making love. He's no slouch at that, either. At one time he had three married women in tow, to whom, in turn, he made love 'with rather cold passion'. Once in a while, usually during the course of a job or after it is all over, he has a somewhat warmer affair with the particular girl he has met while on the case. Of course, he always does meet a girl. No adventure has turned out to be a stag party yet, a fact for which we are extremely grateful.

The girls Bond meets are always attractive, and they almost always succumb to his charms, either sooner or later. Only once, as far as is recorded—not counting Lesbians—has his nose ever been put out of joint. This was accomplished by Gala Brand, a delectable young police-woman who endured dire vicissitudes in his company during the expolit versus Sir Hugo Drax.

SMERSH, the Russian organization, now disbanded, used to have a pretty bulky dossier on James Bond, and he once said that that was one dossier he would certainly like to see. So far, he never has seen it. But we are more fortunate, and have been granted a peep into some of its contents. They give a good thumbnail sketch of the man.

'First name: JAMES. Height: 183 centimetres, weight: 76 kilograms; slim build; eyes: blue; hair: black; scar down right cheek and left shoulder; signs of plastic surgery on back of right hand; all-round athlete; expert pistol shot, boxer, knife-thrower; does not use disguises. Languages: French and German. Smokes heavily (N.B.: special cigarettes with three gold bands);

vices: drink, but not to excess, and women. Not thought to accept bribes.'

A whole page is now skipped, which we resent, and the dossier goes on:

'This man is invariably armed with a .25 Beretta automatic carried in a holster under his left arm. Magazine holds eight rounds. Has been known to carry a knife strapped to his left forearm; has used steel-capped shoes; knows the basic holds of judo. In general, fights with tenacity and has a high tolerance of pain.'

The conclusion runs as follows:

'This man is a dangerous professional terrorist and spy. He has worked for the British Secret Service since 1938 and now (see Highsmith file of December 1950) holds the secret number "007" in that Service. The double 0 numerals signify an agent who has killed and is privileged to kill on active service. There are believed to be only two other British agents with this authority. The fact that this spy was decorated with the C.M.G. in 1953, an award usually given only on retirement from the Secret Service, is a measure of his worth. If encountered in the field, the fact and full details to be reported to headquarters (see SMERSH, M.G.B. and G.R.U. Standing Orders 1951 onward).'

SMERSH also had several photographs of Bond, the best of which seems to be a blown-up copy of his passport photo. 'It was a dark, clean-cut face, with a three inch scar showing whitely down the sunburned skin of the right cheek. The eyes were wide and level under straight, rather long black brows. The hair was black, parted on the left, and carelessly brushed so that a thick black comma fell down over the right eyebrow.' It's something of a trade-mark, that comma, and it gets mentioned in quite a number of the books. 'The longish straight nose ran down to a short upper lip below which was a wide and finely drawn but cruel mouth. The line of the jaw was straight and firm. A section of dark suit, white shirt and black knitted tie completed the picture.'

'He looks a nasty customer,' comments the Russian general scrutinizing the photograph.

We who read Ian Fleming have come to know James Bond's looks very well by this time. But no two of us see him alike, obviously. More than once we have been told that he looks like Hoagy Carmichael when younger. The middle-aged, who knew of, and remember Carmichael as he looked before the war, visualize Bond somewhat differently from those more youthful readers, whose probable introduction to the Secret Service agent was either the glossy pictorial cover of a Pan edition or Sean Connery's film characterization. Hoagy Carmichael's appearance must be relatively unknown to the younger generation: those who do know it see only the collarless, ageing actor with the chamberpot hat who used to be featured in television's 'Laramie'. This must be confusing. We contemporaries of Fleming, of course, see the Carmichael who wrote 'Stardust', and who appeared in those Hollywood films of the 'thirties and 'forties: a very handsome young man indeed. Lately, I've found all this equally confusing. Sean Connery is so good that I begin to wonder nowadays whether or not I didn't always see Bond in his image.

The aforementioned perceptive Domino Vitali, by the way, whose impression of James Bond was much the same as that of the Russian general looking at the passport photo, noted the scar down his right cheek too. But Vivienne Michel, purportedly co-author with Ian Fleming of *The Spy Who Loved Me,* recalled that scar as being down the *left* cheek. This gaffe can't be blamed on Fleming: after all, he was only writing down what Vivienne told him.

James Bond unashamedly enjoys the good things of life. He eats well and he drinks well, and he is a very heavy smoker. He gets through some sixty cigarettes a day—not the Virginian blend, which he hates, but a special brand of a Balkan and Turkish mixture, which are made for him by Morlands of Grosvenor Street, and each of which bears three gold bands. Under great stress or at times of keen concentration he smokes even more. On the second day of his case at the casino in Eaux-les-Royale he smoked seventy. But when he lit that last one it was past three o'clock in the morning. Perhaps we should reckon the last twenty or so as being smoked on a new day?

He has a wide, gunmetal cigarette-case that holds fifty, and he sports a black, oxidised lighter. At the card table he puts them down beside him. It is quite reasonable that he should prefer to smoke his own cigarettes, but not so reasonable that he should resent being offered a light from someone else's match or lighter. On one occasion he took a cigarette from a packet that was held out to him—it was a hated Virginian, by the way—because it seemed policy to do so, but he deliberately refused to see the light that was offered immediately afterwards and he lit the cigarette from his own black Ronson.

Bond is quite aware of his faddy attitude. He says it is pernickety and old-maidish, and he admits to taking a ridiculous pleasure in what he eats and drinks. 'It comes partly from being a bachelor, but mostly from a habit of taking a lot of trouble over details.' This faddiness of his extends to cocktails, and it is very contagious. Even Harold Steptoe, on one occasion, insisted on his Martini being 'shaken, not stirred.'

Bond has strong likes and dislikes when it comes to food and drink. He knows exactly what he wants and he usually asks for it in an abrupt and authoritative way. At home he seldom needs to choose his breakfast—May knows the sort of thing he likes. In hotels he will ring Room Service and rattle off his order for the first meal of the day with something like: 'Scrambled eggs—double portion. Bacon. Black coffee—very hot, in a large cup. Toast. Marmalade. Got it?' In restaurants he allows himself a choice from the menu, but he is no less emphatic. He appreciates good food and he recognizes the best wines. His knowledgeable orders have been known to extract compliments from head waiters.

But 'James Bond was not a gourmet,' we learn in *On Her Majesty's Secret Service* (1963). Now I should have thought that he was. *The Concise Oxford English Dictionary* defines a gourmet as a 'connoisseur of table delicacies, especially of wine.' That definition seems to fit Bond pretty well.

'In England he lived on grilled soles, œufs cocotte and cold roast beef* with potato salad.' It is only when travelling abroad, it seems, usually on his own, that meals become 'something to look forward to, something to break the tension' of his risky spy's existence. But for all this he is blasé about the continental table. He had had it, Fleming informs us. 'He had had the whole lip-smacking ritual of winesmanship and foodsmanship...' This, of course, is in 1963. Well, it has taken James Bond a long time to reach this state of culinary *weltschmerz*. For a good ten years, at least, he has been relishing the mouth-watering meals his creator set before him, and they haven't all been eaten abroad, either. With the possible exception of Thomas Wolfe, who could compose a gastronomic symphony that goes on for pages, I can think of no twentieth century writer, offhand, who even approaches

---

* Asked if he likes beef, in *You Only Live Twice*, ' "No," said Bond stolidly. "As a matter of fact, I don't." ' Admittedly, he's on the defensive at the time, but since he practically lives on the stuff in England, perhaps he's had a surfeit, and is telling the truth.

Ian Fleming in his descriptions of delectable food. Outside of the cookery books, that is.

M, that Spartan advocate of self-discipline and self-denial, who allows himself only two cheroots a day, and who dismisses any drink he doesn't approve of himself as 'rot-gut', invites Bond to Christmas dinner at his home in *On Her Majesty's Secret Service*. It is not wholly a social occasion—they are right in the middle of a big case—otherwise the Secret Service agent would assuredly have dodged this particular meal.

Bond, during the traditional ordeal, is 'aching for a drink'. He receives 'a small glass of very old Marsala and most of a bottle of very bad Algerian wine'. M, apparently, might have been drinking nectar! His palate must have dulled considerably since that evening, several years previously, when he played host to Bond at his club. In fact, Chapter V of *Moonraker*, entitled 'Dinner at Blade's,' is an education. No turkey, plum pudding or Algerian wine here. M starts off with vodka. No inferior stuff, of course. 'This is real pre-war Wolfschmidt from Riga.' Bond approves.

> 'Then what?' asked M. 'Champagne? Personally, I'm going to have a half-bottle of claret. The Mouton Rothschild '34, please, Grimley. But don't pay any attention to me, James. I'm an old man. Champagne's no good for me. We've got some good champagnes, haven't we, Grimley? None of that stuff you're always telling me about, I'm afraid, James. Don't often see it in England. Taittinger, wasn't it?'

Bond leaves the choice to Grimley, the wine steward, who suggests the Dom Perignon '46. It's hard to come by: France only sells it for dollars, but this is a gift from the Regency Club in New York.

When the vodka arrives, the fastidious Bond grins that he 'shouldn't have insulted the club Wolfschmidt' but he nevertheless sprinkles a pinch of black pepper on to the surface of his vodka to take the poisonous fusel oil to the bottom. 'In Russia, where you get a lot of bath-tub liquor, it's an understood thing to sprinkle a little pepper into your glass... now it's a habit.' M doesn't particularly mind, as long as Bond doesn't do the same thing with the champagne.

To eat, M begins with a new delivery of Beluga caviar. Bond plumps for smoked salmon, for which he confesses he has a mania when it's really good. M orders devilled kidney and a slice of bacon, with peas and new potatoes, followed by strawberries in kirsch. Bond wastes no time in choosing

His Image

lamb cutlets. He takes the same vegetables as M, 'as it's May,' and admits that asparagus 'with Bearnaise sauce sounds wonderful. And perhaps a slice of pineapple.'

'Thank heaven for a man who makes up his mind,' is M's remark.

He should be as privileged as we are to accompany Bond on his adventures. This was no exception. Our man knows *exactly* what he wants, *always*, whether he is reading from a restaurant menu or delivering one of those staccato orders over the telephone in some hotel in France, Turkey or Jamaica.

M winds up his meal with a marrow bone, one of 'half a dozen in today from the country,' which has been specially kept in case he came in. M can't resist them, although he admits they are bad for him.

James Bond and his host glide effortlessly through this meal, with we armchair observers salivating enviously. Bond's smoked salmon has 'the glutinous texture only achieved by the Highland cures—very different from the dessicated products of Scandinavia.' Asked how his cutlets were, Bond rates them superb. 'I could cut them with a fork. The best English cooking is the best in the world—particularly at this time of the year.'

Apropos the champagne and claret, the two diners go through the solemn observance of delivering a favourable judgment on the wines, despite the 'lip-smacking ritual of winesmanship' that Bond is to deprecate some years later. Without apology, he tips Benzedrine into his glass, and earns M's impatient query for the reason. But it's all in the line of duty. Bond needs a clear head for the ordeal to come. This meal, described over nine and a half pages, with conversation and quiet observations, is only a fortification for the main business of the evening: exposing Sir Hugo Drax as a cheat at cards.

The pair finish off with coffee and brandy in the card room. Bond and M definitely appreciated good food in those days, even if one now drinks bad Algerian wine and the other is not a gourmet.

One thing seems certain: Ian Fleming is. But *he* doesn't think so. Geoffrey Bocca, in an interview,* tells us: 'Fleming protests constantly that he is not a gourmet like James Bond.' Something wrong here: less than a year earlier Fleming had told us that Bond was *not* a gourmet!

I shouldn't think he has very many friends. We are seldom told about any. I mean coves corresponding to people like

* 'Profile of Ian Fleming', in *Modern Woman*, December 1963.

Algy Longworth, Peter Darrell, Richard Chandos and Sandy Arbuthnot of clubland. He does get on pretty well with Felix Leiter, that unfortunate American shamus, whenever they happen to meet on a job—and this means almost every time Bond is occupied west of the shores of England—but they are hardly more than drinking companions when not engaged in mayhem. Much of their leisure together seems confined to ribbing each other about their choice in cars and to talk of food and drink. I imagine that they would soon sicken of each other's company if they had a great deal of it. For that matter, come to think of it, Bond would soon sicken of *anyone's* company, male or female.

He seems to be essentially the lone wolf, and yet this term is completely inadequate. It tends to give quite the wrong impression. Bond may have no close friends that we know of, but he is far from being a solitary. He possesses all the social graces, he has a natural charm, he can be companionable enough when he likes, and he would never need to wander through life unloved and unwanted. I suspect that he would despise most of the back-slapping hearties with whom he might tend to come into contact if he made an effort to become a little more gregarious. He's probably better off the way he is. He confines himself to occasional lunches with Bill, the Chief of Staff at Universal Export, and probably a binge with one of the other 00 boys when any of them return after a tough assignment. Bond is definitely a ladies' man rather than a man's man. He is inclined to put up with any old maudlin chat from a girl if it looks as if there might be something in it for James, but he is less disposed to intimate conversation with men.

We are told that he doesn't like personal questions. Well, he must have had enough of them in his time. What woman can refrain from asking them? And he's certainly had enough women. Perhaps he only dislikes personal questions from men?

At one state in the saga it is pointed out that he has no wife or children and has never suffered a personal loss. We don't know the full strength of it, but it seems probable that he might have been orphaned in childhood, too young to fully understand. Either that, or his old Mum and Dad rusticate to this day up in Glencoe. For the time being, we don't know.* What we do know is that things are a little bit different since it was written that he had never suffered a personal loss. Now, he *has*.

Although Bond is the perennial bachelor, the idea of

---

* We do now, thanks to 'Obit:'. His parents were killed in a climbing accident when he was eleven.

His Image

marriage crosses his mind more and more frequently with the passing years. He *says* that he always thought that if ever he married it would be to an air hostess. When he is asked why he first of all says that he doesn't know, but he goes on to explain quite explicitly. 'It would be fine to have a girl always tucking you up and bringing you hot meals and asking if you had everything you wanted. And they're always smiling and wanting to please. If I don't find an air hostess, there'll be nothing for it but to marry a Japanese. They seem to have the right idea, too.' But he's really only making conversation. He 'had no intention of marrying anyone. If he did it would certainly not be to an insipid slave.' And yet this sort of fantasy obviously appeals to him. At a later date, admittedly at a time when he is not wholly himself, the idea of marrying and settling down with a ministering angel who brings him a glass of brandy crosses his fuddled mind.

In 1953, dealing with Jonah Mansel, Richard Usborne wrote the following:

> Jonah is perhaps the bossiest hero in thriller-fiction since Sherlock Holmes. Irene Adler might have softened Holmes up if she had ever become Mrs. Holmes. If Jonah ever marries, his wife will be hard put to it to find anything to do round the house. Jonah will boss the servants, boss the house and arrange their holidays to suit his fishing and his chasing of crooks. He may allow his wife to run the garden.

Well, I concede that Mansel may still hold the title of the bossiest, but I claim James Bond as the fussiest and the most meticulous. After twenty-odd years of adult bachelorhood, I can't see him knuckling down to *any* woman. It's all very well for him to go nest-building, as he does on one occasion, but men do funny things when they're in love. If Bond ever settles down, once the gilt has worn off the gingerbread there will be ructions.

Take furniture, for instance. Women, and particularly newly-married women, have pretty strong ideas about how they would like their homes to be. 'Comfy', would, I think, be the appropriate word, and one that most of them might use. But comfort to James Bond has a very different meaning, in this context, to that understood by the majority of girls. I recall him sitting on a chintzy sofa in a drawing-room with the Governor of the Bahamas in a somewhat off-beat story called 'Quantam of Solace'.

... Bond had a sharp sense of the ridiculous. He was

never comfortable sitting deep in soft cushions. He preferred to sit up in a solidly upholstered armed chair with his feet firmly on the ground. And he felt foolish sitting with an elderly bachelor on this bed of rose chintz gazing at the coffee and liqueurs on the low table between their outstretched feet. There was something clubable, intimate, even rather feminine, about the scene and none of these atmospheres was appropriate.

Well, I don't necessarily insist that Tracy di Vicenso would have plumped for this sort of furnishing: it's difficult to know what the hell she *would* have liked, but I'll bet Tiffany Case's taste would have leant in this direction, and with a Kewpie doll stuck on top of the sofa, too! And these two lovelies got nearer than anyone else to settling down with Bond in a permanent love nest.

There's another thing: what about May? She's never going to take orders from some long-leggity, proud-bosomed strumpet from foreign parts. If the worst comes to the worst and Bond does ever carry a bride over the threshold of that Chelsea flat, it's a safe bet that ere long May will have packed her bags and flounced off back to Glen Orchy. And never forget that in England Bond practically lives on grilled soles and cold roast beef. A Tiffany type is going to make an attractive picture in the kitchen, but sooner or later she's going to start experimenting with a few other dishes. I'd say that it would be about a month at the outside before James Bond despatched an urgent telegram to Glen Orchy and, in the same single swift movement, placed the sole of one of his casuals firmly upon a delectable *derrière* and propelled its owner on to the pavement of a tree-lined square in Chelsea.

No, I just can't conceive connubiality for Bond. It's all very well for him to go dreaming up fantasies about air hostesses and Japanese girls and then telling himself that he would never marry an insipid slave. The truth of the matter is that such a woman is the only type that Bond could possibly live with for more than a week or two.*

He appears to have only one serious hobby: fast cars. The earliest of these that we know about, and most certainly the first one he ever owned, was 'one of the last of the 4½ litre Bentleys with the supercharger by Amherst Villiers.' He bought it in 1933. Harping back to this business of his age, if it is established that Bond was about twenty-six at the end of the war, he bought that car at the age of fourteen! On the other hand, if he was still only about thirty-six in 1961, as Domino guesses him to be, he was about eight years old

* *Vide* Kissy Suzuki in *You Only Live Twice*.

His Image

when he bought his first car. Since he 'had kept it in careful storage through the war', either he was waiting till he was old enough to buy a licence or he was serving his country and lied about his age.

Ian Fleming, whose success, to a large extent, must be attributed to the verisimilitude in the stories—points about Bond's appearance, clothes, likes and dislikes—appears to have boobed in establishing the man's age. Of course, we know without any doubt that in many respects Fleming and Bond are one and the same person. They may not look alike and they may not act alike, but they are both Commanders and they were both in the R.N.V.R. When Fleming tells us of Bond's preferences and prejudices he is more often than not probably describing his own. But Fleming is by some years the older man of the two, and it is a reasonable guess that it was he who bought the Bentley in 1933 and he who stored it so carefully during the war.

At any rate, Bond still had this car twenty years after he acquired it. In *Live and Let Die* (1954), he is still running it. But the following year, in *Moonraker*, chasing Drax down the Dover Road at break-neck speed, he smashes up his beloved Bentley under circumstances that might be termed unusual. The villain slows down behind a lorry carrying twenty enormous rolls of newsprint—some fourteen tons— and instructs his henchman to climb aboard and cut the ropes that hold them. Drax's timing and steering in avoiding the rolls as they pour off the lorry and down a one-in-ten gradient is masterly. The quality of the pursuing Bond's driving is quite understandably less so. He got away with his life, of course, but the Bentley was a write-off.

We cannot believe that Bond was very long without another car,* but for the next few years we are privileged to find him driving only a D.B. III, 'from the pool'. We learn that he could have had the Aston Martin or a Jaguar 3.4 for the job on hand, either of which 'would have suited his cover', but he chooses the D.B. III because of numerous extras it bears, not the least of which are a gun in a trick compartment under the driving seat and lots of 'concealed space that would fox the customs men.'

Fleming appears to know his Dornford Yates. Jonah

---

* On page 253 of the original edition of *Moonraker*, Bond is after a 1953 Mark VI with an open touring body. It's battleship grey, like the old 4½-litre. 'She's sold. On one condition. That you get her over to the ferry terminal at Calais by tomorrow evening.' Presumably the test driver fulfilled his part of the bargain: Bond's plans came unstuck. I wonder what happened to that Mark VI?

Mansel owned such a car, but one with extras which surpassed the D.B. III. That little job even had a concealed compartment which housed Mansel's dog at the crucial moments when he was crossing to and from the Continent.

For five years or so, apart from the D.B. III, we only find Bond taking taxis or being given lifts. But by 1961, in *Thunderball*, he owns 'the most selfish car in England. It was a Mark II Continental Bentley that some rich idiot had married to a telegraph pole on the Great West Road. Bond had bought the bits for £1,500 and Rolls had straightened the bend in the chassis and fitted new clockwork—the Mark IV engine with 9.5 compression.' We are given the better part of a page describing the unusual features of the car, which he calls his locomotive. 'A car, however splendid, was a means of locomotion ... and it must at all times be ready to locomote—no garage doors to break one's nails on, no pampering with mechanics except for the quick monthly service.' He keeps it out of doors in front of his flat.

Bond has changed since the old Eaux-les-Royale days, with the 4½ litre Bentley. Then, 'a former Bentley mechanic, who worked in a garage near Bond's Chelsea flat, tended it with jealous care.' He also kept it under cover.

Particular as he is about his car, his food and his drink, James Bond is no less particular about the clothes he wears. Throughout the books these are described in great detail. It would be interesting to get a dozen or so avid Fleming readers on to various psychiatrists' couches and have the popularly accepted jargon fed to them. I visualize the scene.

'I'm going to mention a few things: objects, names, places. I want you to tell me the first thing that comes into your mind. Do you understand?'

'Yes.'

'Right ... James Bond.'

Now I haven't tried this personally, and I don't know any psychiatrists well enough to enlist their aid, but I'd still be willing to bet that for every subject whose first reply would be 'Ian Fleming' or some variation on the 'sex, sadism and snobbery' theme there would be another who muttered about black, knitted silk ties or sea island shirts. I'd also guess that the sale of these items of apparel has increased considerably in the past few years.

Although I had never heard of sea island shirts until Fleming started writing about them, today I own one. Asked what I wanted as a gift from a friend returning from Jamaica, there was only one answer. I knew I could never have Solitaire or Honeychile Rider. This was

His Image

the nearest I would ever get to being like James Bond.

Two of my copies of the early Bond books are second-hand. A previous owner, as meticulous in his own way as Ian Fleming is in his, summed up the books he bought and read in one pencilled sentence on the title pages. The first says: 'A wardrobe author'; the second remarks: 'More wardrobe and restaurant'. Perhaps this is less than fair, but no one could deny the element of truth in these brief summaries. There *is* emphasis in these delightful books on food and clothes. Fleming denies that Bond is a gourmet, however, and apparently he would not have us think that his man is vain.

Bond accepts a Russian agent, a SMERSH employee, as being a British Secret Service man in *From Russia, With Love*. But he distrusts the chap because of a Windsor knot in his tie. To Bond, this smacks of too much vanity. Apparently it is vain to sport a knot which to the wearer is more aesthetically pleasing than the conventional one, but it is *not* vain to wear dark blue, sea island shirts without sleeves, or to affect black, knitted silk ties.

Surely, once Bond has tied his tie before the mirror and has assured himself of its set and has experienced the brief satisfaction of seeing it, for the rest of the day it is to be viewed mostly by the people with whom he is to come into contact? And surely he wears what he does wear for the effect on others and because he thinks it suits him? If there is the minimum of vanity in Bond's own makeup, why is he then so meticulous about the clothes he puts on? Comfort plays a large part, admittedly. His compromise in wearing only pyjama tops with no trousers, is fully acceptable and understandable. The same goes for sleeveless shirts, if he finds them comfortable. But why must they always be blue, and dark blue at that? Similarly, a shantung tie or an ordinary cotton one is no more and no less comfortable than a knitted, silk one. In addition, it is difficult for us to believe that Bond is so different from the rest of us that he has never been afflicted by gifts of innumerable variegated items of neckwear at Christmas. There are certainly enough feminine admirers in his life: the primary offenders in this respect. Why doesn't he select from his wardrobe each morning the first tie that comes to hand, provided it's not too outrageous? Why his insistence always on the black, knitted silk sort? In my opinion, only because he thinks he looks good in them. To James Bond they are aesthetically satisfactory. I think he is just as vain about his own neckwear as the SMERSH agent was about his.

Perhaps other people distrust *Bond?* I feel sure that M has noticed those black, knitted ties, even if he's never said anything.

It's worth noting, in passing, that M himself is inclined to favour the bow tie. Anyone thinking of James Bond as a complete replica of his creator should beware. He isn't. And there are bits of Fleming in some of the *other* characters, as well. That bow tie, for instance. According to Geoffrey Bocca, a spotted bow has been standard with Fleming since he was demobilized. Most photographs will bear this out. Of course, he does wear blue, sea island shirts without sleeves (pure Bond), because 'I cannot stand dirty shirt cuffs,' and he prefers casual shoes (also Bond, who can't bear shoe laces), but rather surprisingly his suits have cuffs on the sleeves, a nicety which Bond would never affect. I say never—I tell a lie. There was one occasion when he had to pass himself off as Sir Hilary Bray, in *On Her Majesty's Secret Service*.

'And who the hell are *you* supposed to be?' is M's initial query to this subterfuge. Bond is quite a bit embarrassed at having to explain. He's to be an emissary from the College of Arms, and he's doing his best to act the part. Having been briefed by a specialist in genealogy with the unlikely name of Sable Basilisk, Bond swots for some weeks on the subject of heraldry, and he eventually emerges with a new background and personality. He informs his secretary that he's got 'two new suits with cuffs and double vents at the back and four buttons down the front ... Quite the little baronet.' Fleming actually dedicates this book to two people named as Sable Basilisk Pursuivant and Hilary Bray, 'who came to the aid of the party, and it is clear that he owed them much, whoever they are, in his effort at verisimilitude and search for local colour. But it is also clear that he was taking the mickey out of himself just a little in building this false character for Bond.

Life is not all food and drink, fast cars and smart clothes for the Secret Service agent, by any means. He does a job, too—a job which would have most of us inside a hospital or a nursing-home with a nervous breakdown within a week or two. This is assuming that we could live through that week or two, something which is by no means a certainty. He takes his life in his hands every time he goes off on an assignment. It is fifty-fifty that he will never come back and he knows it very well. He is not particularly bothered by the knowledge that his gaurdian angel has hovered close to him for a long, long time and is about due for a spell off duty.

He feels pretty sure that his luck will run out one day, but flirting with danger is as necessary to him as is smoking a cigarette. He likes his work in the double-O Section and he resents the slightest hint that it might be getting too much for him.

James Bond is a trained professional killer: it's no use beating about the bush with euphemisms. He kills as a soldier will kill; 'in the field', destroying his enemies in the name of his queen and his country. He will fight hand to hand if he finds it expedient to do so, or he will kill with a sniper's bullet if it is not. He has long ago discarded any public-school sentiments about fair play and sporting chances. He has killed in hot and in cold blood, but he is very different from the hired hoodlums of gangland, who will murder a man they have never known or seen before as dispassionately as they will step on an insect, or who will snuff out a life 'just for kicks'. Violent death, of which he has seen and meted out so much, has never given him pleasure—or any great pain, for that matter.

> It was part of his profession to kill people. He had never liked doing it and when he had to kill he did it as well as he knew how and forgot about it. As a secret agent who held the rare double-O prefix—a licence to kill in the Secret Service—it was his duty to be as cool about death as a surgeon. If it happened, it happened. Regret was unprofessional—worse, it was a death-watch beetle in the soul.

He is as tough and as accomplished as a commando—probably more so: he has been going longer than any commando did, actively. He is muscular, but he is not a particularly strong man, in the way that Bulldog Drummond was strong. But Bond is infinitely more scientific: he is the rapier rather than the bludgeon. He can kill with a chop of his hand and with the well-placed pressure of his fingers. He knows how to use knives and he knows how to use razors. Most of all, he knows how to use guns.

Bond likes firearms. He is quite happy with a pistol and a tiny target in the basement at Universal Export and just as happy with a rifle on the range at Bisley. He has carried a gun in a holster under his armpit for so long that he would probably feel only half-dressed without it.

In *Casino Royale,* during the earliest of his exploits that we know about, he slips his hand under the pillow round a .38 Colt Police Positive. He keeps this by him as a possible safeguard against things that go whump in the night. But for everyday use, so to speak, in his holster of light chamois leather he wears a flat .25 Beretta with a skeleton grip. Bond used this weapon for fifteen years, and he got quite fond of it. He might be using it still but for a slip-up he made in *From Russia, With Love*. His silencer got caught in his holster, and it very nearly cost him his life. After that, M turned thumbs down on the Beretta. Major Boothroyd, the Service Armourer, calls it a ladies' gun. At the start of *Dr. No* he recommends a Walther PPK 7.65 mm., to be worn in a Berns Martin Triple-draw holster.* For heavier use he plumps for a Smith and Wesson Centennial Airweight revolver, .38 calibre.

Bond doesn't like the idea of changing from his old Beretta and the Colt, but it's orders, and that's that. He carries the Smith and Wesson with him into the enemy camp, but he never gets much chance to use it. The odds against him this time are far too great. But he scrapes through without it, and at the completion of his assignment he cables M a message in cipher that finishes with a gibe: 'REGRET MUST AGAIN REQUEST SICK LEAVE STOP SURGEONS REPORT FOLLOWS STOP KINDLY INFORM ARMOURER SMITH AND WESSON INEFFECTIVE AGAINST FLAME-THROWER ENDIT.' But he's sorry about it afterwards, as well as he might be. It isn't fair comment. His Colt or his Beretta could have done no better.

In 'From a View to a Kill' (1960), he is using a .45 Colt, but I have suggested earlier that these 'Five Secret Occasions in the Life of James Bond' may not have happened in strict chronological sequence. His use of a Colt here strengthens this assumption. But in 'For Your Eyes Only', published at the same time, he is carrying the Walther PPK, and knowledge of this fact gives us an idea of the time that this adventure took place. But he actually *uses* a rifle in this story. It is one of the 'new Savage 99Fs, Weatherby 6 x 62 'scope, five-shot repeater with twenty rounds of high-velocity .250-3.000.' I have only the vaguest idea of what this means, myself, but it certainly sounds impressive. He needs something good on this occasion: he is after big game—big game in the form of a particularly nasty ex-Gestapo man.

On reflection, I suppose that there is considerable preoccupation with firearms throughout all the books, but no more than with food, drink and fast cars. Most definitely there is less preoccupation with guns than with girls. They trip through these entertaining absurdities of Ian Fleming's with a

---

* I notice that this becomes a Burns-Martin in later books. It isn't a bit like Fleming to make mistakes in details of this sort. Probably a misprint.

regularity that can never grow monotonous. They have their part in the James Bond image just as much as his scrambled eggs at breakfast, his holstered gun, his sea island shirts and his car. But whereas all these things are stable and permanent, the women are transient, fleeting and infinitely varied. But they are as real, as individual and as memorable as James Bond himself. They merit far more than a brief, passing mention of their existence. They have, in fact, contributed largely towards Bond's present popularity. All the world loves a lover, says the no less popular misquotation. I move that it now be stricken from the records and that a mandatory, if maladroit monstrosity be substituted in its stead (back-dated to 1953). 'All the world loves the ladies this lecher loves-up.'

His Women

OFFHAND, I CAN think of no character in fiction so lucky in love as James Bond. Almost every personable female he meets seems more than ready to hop into bed with him at his merest nod. Waitresses brush against him provocatively, married women appear to be his for the asking, other men's mistresses forget their lovers when they see him, and even expensive whores are willing to bestow their favours *pour amour*. Unattached young bachelor girls, of course, are sitting ducks.

Occasionally, though, he meets a girl who has no immediate intention—or eventual intention, for that matter—of copulating with him. More often than not he wins her over. This is usually accomplished by derring-do. What normal girl, or even abnormal girl, can resist him after he has saved her life or gone through some fantastic and harrowing experience with her?

Ian Fleming is so accomplished a yarn-spinner that we can believe all this as easily as we can believe almost everything else Bond gets up to. We enjoy reading our favourite spy's affairs because this side of his life is what each of us, in his heart, would like ours to be. Man is polygamous, perhaps promiscuous, even if only in the mind.

Yes, we accept Bonds loves with hardly any difficulty at all. Only one thing about them strikes a jarring note for me: he is not *quite* true to life in winning his numerous sexual favours. For about twenty-five percent of a woman's life between puberty and the menopause she is unavailable, even to a James Bond. Surely the law of averages demands that he should meet one or two at this time of the month? He is indeed lucky in love. If only he were half as lucky at the card table or at the roulette wheel!

Bond is a quite unashamed cad when it comes to love and women. This may not be admirable, but his accomplishments are. No less admirable than his ability to attract and win desirable women is his way of quietly discarding them when they become, or look like becoming, an encumbrance. From book to book, and from story to story, he gets new girls. Does he never look up an old flame? I wonder what happened to Solitaire after that fortnight's idyll, for instance, back in 1954? Initiated into the delights of love, it is to be hoped that somewhere in Haiti, Jamaica or the States she is happy, and is making some other man, or men, equally happy.

This sort of behaviour with women on Bond's part would never do—need it be said?—for the Terrible Trio between the wars. Hannay, Drummond and Mansel lived in a never-never land where acts of pettiness, untruth, dishonesty and sexual immorality are made only by the villains or the unsympathetic characters. These heroes and those in their immediate circle appeared to be wholly free of the more common human frailities and weaknesses. They seemed incapable, even, of base thoughts, however fleeting. Drummond, it is true, might have made a ribald remark on occasion, but we were seldom given its details. In any case, he meant nothing nasty by it. He only did it to shock, and what he said was really Good Clean Fun. The trio might, at times, have so far forgotten themselves as to utter an expletive, but if it was before a woman it was hardly ever stronger than 'damn' or 'the devil'.

Both Hannay and Drummond married, so presumably what sexual appetites they possessed were appeased along with their other and more mentionable appetites in the day-to-day bliss of connubial existence. Mansel, though, was the perennial bachelor. Dornford Yates has suggested that one time in Jonah's life there was a grand passion, and we are led to believe that it was touch and go with him for a time. But he wavered only on that single occasion. For all we are told about any other women in his life, in the more intimate sense, or his thoughts in that direction, he lived a completely celibate existence. Now monks and suchlike eccentrics must find this sort of life difficult enough, with the minimum of stimulation, temptation and distraction. How Jonah Mansel ever managed to keep Satan behind him is a mystery. That he apparently did speaks worlds for his self-discipline and iron control.

Either this is the answer or else he led a double life, with the Mr. Hyde part of him a secret even from Dornford Yates.

James Bond, however, is far more human than that illustrious triumvirate. He is therefore a far more credible character. Devotee though he may be of the cold shower, and professed hater of the soft life as he is, he equips himself very well in the boudoir. He loves amorous dalliance almost as much as he loves his gun, his vodka and his sea island shirts. Maybe more.

We are told that M strongly disapproves of Bond's womanizing. This isn't surprising: M is not only of round about the same age as Drummond and Mansel—if they're still alive—he might have been at school with them. He almost certainly read John Buchan when he was younger. Sapper and Dornford Yates he might possibly have thought too trashy,* but Lt.-Col. H. C. MacNeile and Maj. William Mercer (the real names of the two private gentlemen who hid behind those *noms-de-plume*) would have been his blood brothers. In fact, M is so near to being a Clubland Hero type himself that in Ian Fleming's hands he becomes almost a caricature of that *genre*.

Although I don't think that Fleming has very often told us specifically the sort of woman James Bond prefers, it isn't difficult to judge his 'type'. Of course, almost without exception the girls in the books are fresh, young and sexually exciting, but such a description is much too general.

Fleming informs us that most of them have short, unpainted fingernails. Since the author goes to such lengths to describe so small a point about his heroines, and since he obviously dislikes long, painted fingernails himself,† it may be taken for granted that James Bond is in complete agreement with him.

Fleming also seems to be very fond of thick, three-inch leather belts about slim waists, and he has a decided preference for striped blouses and flared skirts. In addition, most of the girls with whom Bond gets mixed up seem to deviate slightly from the norm. You can't say that there is always a touch of perversion about them—that is far too strong—and aberration isn't quite the word, either, but there is something a bit queer about the majority of them. This divergence

---

* Not absolutely certain. Somewhat surprisingly, we learn that he reads Rex Stout. Not nearly so surprisingly, though, he doesn't exactly approve of Nero Wolfe. But he grudgingly admits that the books are 'readable'.

† He lays his predilection on a bit thick with Kissy, his latest: '... her finger-nails and toe-nails, although they were cut very short, were broken. Bond found this rather endearing.'

ranges from some physical peculiarity to a mental quirk. Honey, for instance, is a magnificent Venus, but she has a broken nose; Tiffany exudes sex, but she had had an unfortunate experience in her youth and will let no man touch her. This only makes her more desirable, and she surrenders to Bond in the end. Solitaire, as her name implies, is an ungregarious and misogamistic beauty—for the nonce—while Pussy Galore is a frank and quite unashamed Lesbian. It takes a Bond to turn her heterosexual. Vivienne Michel is a bit of a 'query' too, though in a different way. How many girls would have Told All.—'It's all true—absolutely,'—to her co-author, Mr. Fleming? As for Tracy, well, she's the oddest of the lot. Is this why Bond takes her more seriously than the rest?

As a sort of counterpoint to the main erotic themes that run through these fascinating movements in the symphony of James Bond there is a subsidiary haunting and tantalizing melody in a minor key which never quite resolves. It takes place in the corridors and quiet offices of Universal Export.

Periodically, we are told, Bond and the other two members of the 00 Section attempted to seduce their secretary, Loelia Ponsonby, who is described as being 'tall and dark with a reserved, unbroken beauty', but with 'a touch of sternness'. Reading between the lines, it looks to the observer as if Bond wouldn't encounter very much opposition if he really and truly 'made determined assaults on her virtue' as he and his 00 colleagues are described as doing. Knowing Bond as we do, I feel that he is being somewhat circumspect with regard to Loelia. After all, there is an old tag involving one's own doorstep which he has surely heard and is more than probably acting upon.

Anyway, the whole thing is in abeyance at the moment. The rather stern Loelia, who had hitherto seemingly led the life of a nun, has now left the Service, and she is married. Her husband is 'dull, but worthy'. Sour grapes? Maybe, maybe not. But she's not on James Bond's doorstep now, so married or not, she'd better look out if ever she runs into him accidentally.

Her replacement, a former Wren named Mary Goodnight, looks like emulating Loelia as a permanent tease to the 00 boys. These adventurers have a wager on regarding which of them will reach home first. Bond was co-favourite for a time, but so far no-one has got to first base.

Another charmer at Universal Export is M's private secretary, Miss Moneypenny. Back in *Casino Royale* (1953), she 'would have been desirable but for her eyes which were cool and direct and quizzical.' A year later, in *Live and Let Die*, we hear nothing about her eyes. She is the 'desirable

Miss Moneypenny'. In *Diamonds Are Forever*, the following year, Bond smiles into her 'warm brown eyes'. By *From Russia, With Love* (1957), those eyes have 'that old look of excitement and secret knowledge' as she passes him through to M. In *Goldfinger* (1959), she is still desirable. *Thunderball* (1961) finds her warming up considerably. By this time she 'often dreamed hopelessly about Bond,' but he—the daft clot —doesn't seem to notice.

Ah, well. The Miss Moneypenny of the books is doing the best she can and not getting very far. Her counterpart in the films, though, makes things a teeny bit more obvious. Naturally, this medium is far more expressive, but Bond doesn't quite rise to the bait. He hasn't got the time, anyway. Whether in print or on celluloid, the only occasions on which he seems to see her are during fleeting visits to M's office for a quick briefing. Then he's off to foreign parts, more often than not, and any promising thoughts he might have entertained about Penny are very soon dispelled by a confrontation with a new adversary or a fresh feminine distraction.

If he *really* wants a soul-mate, which I beg leave to doubt, I don't think he will ever find one among those exotic bints he is forever running up against in foreign countries. His best bet is quite obviously some sort of compromise between the efficient, statuesque air hostess (brains and beauty)—and the Japanese fantasy—(they also serve who only lie and wait). He should seek that compromise within the purlieus of the Regent's Park area. He could go farther and fare a lot worse.

The first of James Bond's conquests that we are privileged to witness is that of Vesper Lynd. Without the slightest doubt he had had many affairs long before this one,[*] but since we know very little about them this brief romance with Vesper takes on the aspect, almost, of first love.

Like him, she is a Secret Service Agent, and a very glamorous one. She is blue-eyed and black-haired. Although she exudes femininity she is not fussy, as most girls would be, with her low, heavy hair, which is on the move with every shift of her head. This is a subtle Fleming touch, one of the first we get, betraying his predilections. No, 'she did not constantly pat it back into place, but let it alone.' Hard on the heels of this touch come two more. 'Her skin was lightly

[*] Bond lost his virginity, together with his wallet, at the age of sixteen, in Paris. If Ian Fleming is ever stumped for an idea for a short story, out of sequence, I humbly suggest that he elaborates on this incident. He will earn my undying gratitude if he does, and that of many others, I most earnestly assure him.

suntanned and bore no trace of make-up except on her mouth which was wide and sensual.' Her finger-nails are 'unpainted and cut short.'

She wears a hand-stitched black belt three inches thick, a pleated skirt, and clothes which show off her figure well. Oh yes, her shoes are square-toed and plain. Bond is immediately attracted. She likes him, too. When they are having dinner together she confesses that she was enchanted when she learned that she was to work with a Double 0. 'Of course, you're our heroes.' He's halfway there already.

Her briefing, by her boss, the Head of S, had been dampening. He knows Bond very well, of course, as we are to get to know him over the next few years, and he had given her a warning. 'Don't imagine this is going to be any fun. He thinks of nothing but the job on hand and, while it's on he's absolute hell to work for... He's a good-looking chap, but don't fall for him. I don't think he's got much heart. Anyway, good luck and don't get hurt.'

Vesper does get hurt. She gets hurt both physically and emotionally. Bond, on the other hand, suffers tortures only to his body: tortures so extreme that they lay the firm foundation of the charges of sadism that have since been regularly made against Ian Fleming.

About halfway through the book, when it looks as if Bond's mission is successfully completed, he relaxes a bit and allows himself a few cruel thoughts about Vesper. He wonders about her morals. 'He wanted her cold and arrogant body. He wanted to see tears and desire in her remote blue eyes and to take the ropes of her black hair in his hands and bend her long body back under his.' The rotten cad.

That night things look quite rosy for a bit, but within a very short time things go awry. Vesper is kidnapped by Le Chiffre, the villain, and is bundled into the back seat of a car. The gunman guarding her has made his job easy in a most original way: 'Apart from her legs, which were naked to the hips, Vesper was only a parcel. Her long black velvet skirt had been lifted over her arms and head and tied above her head with a piece of rope.' No stockings or underclothes?

Bond gives chase, but that's exactly what Le Chiffre wants. He empties a load of spiked chain-mail from the boot of his car, and the Secret Service man, coming up behind, speeds straight into it. Within seconds Bond's car has crashed and he is an unconscious captive. But he comes to before they all reach their destination: Le Chiffre's villa. Vesper, 'looking incredibly indecent in the early light of day,' as well she might, is taken inside with him.

There now follows the diabolical torture scene, aforementioned, which only a James Bond could survive. Survive he does, although his recuperation is naturally slow and painful, but Vesper is never very far away, and he looks to be finally over the hump when he is sufficiently interested to ask to see her. His mind stirs with erotic thoughts of her and he recalls her indecent nakedness at the villa.

But, while recovering, it is touch and go whether he will ever be able to make love again. Almost recovered, he is afraid. 'Afraid that his senses and his body would not respond to her sensual beauty. Afraid that he would feel no stir of desire and that his blood would stay cool.' He need not have worried. When recovery is complete their affair is out of this world. He is in love. 'That day he would ask Vesper to marry him. He was quite certain. It was only a question of choosing the right moment.'

It is at this point in the story that one begins to wonder if Ian Fleming didn't realize that he had got a winner on his hands with *Casino Royale*. Should he marry Bond off? Sapper hog-tied Bulldog Drummond in his very first adventure, and he found *himself* hog-tied, from then on, as far as writing about romance was concerned. Not that Drummond would have got up to the tricks that we have come to expect from Bond. Such things were Not Done.

Perhaps Fleming foresaw many more James Bond exploits, even at this early stage, or perhaps a discerning publisher's reader did? At any rate, at this point the tale takes a disconcerting twist. Vesper turns out to be a double agent. She has been blackmailed into working for Russia as well as for Britain. She commits suicide.

'His eyes were wet and he dried them.' Getting through to London, Bond is once more 007, the hard, cruel, secret agent, reporting on an open line—as it's an emergency. 'Can you hear me? Pass this on at once. 3030 was a double, working for Redland.'

The book ends with a masterly touch, summarizing James Bond in two terse sentences: ' "Yes, dammit, I said "was". The bitch is dead now." '

Did I say that he was only tortured physically?

Solitaire, the next girl Bond meets in the line of duty, is 'one of the most beautiful women' he had ever seen. She turns up a year later, in *Live and Let Die*. Vesper Lynd had been fairly normal, but Solitaire is anything but that. She is the first of the female weirdies who march regularly through the Bond books.

Her real name is Simone Latrelle. She was born in Haiti, and she is telepathic. She is very pale, she has blue eyes, her long, heavy hair is blue-black, and she has a sensual mouth. She doesn't wear rings and her nails are 'short and without enamel.' Obviously, Bond is immediately attracted.

She appears to be a virgin. Although living in a form of semi-captivity under the protection of Mr. Big, an enormous and diabolic Negro gangster, who is also a SMERSH agent, her virtue remains intact. He intends to marry her, presumably to further the science of eugenics. As he says, it will be interesting to see their children. 'For the time being she is difficult. She will have nothing to do with men.'

She hadn't seen Bond till now, of course. This makes all the difference. Within seconds of meeting the agent, who is Mr. Big's captive at the time, she sits down 'almost touching his right knee.' Very soon afterwards she gives him the old come-on. She 'nonchalantly drew her forearms together in her lap so that the valley between her breasts deepened.'

This man Bond certainly has something that we don't possess. As Fleming informs us, the message is unmistakable.

Although Solitaire has been enlisted by Mr. Big to read the Secret Service man's mind, and to say whether or not he is lying, Bond's charm wins him an immediate ally. She looks to be on his side from the start. This is without a single overture in any way from him. He is strapped to a chair at the time, anyway, and he couldn't do much, even if he wanted to. He has a concealed gun poing at him, too, and Mr. Big is watching his every move. The gangster even notices the slight response which shows on Bond's face at Solitaire's sexy message, and he soon puts a stop to any further nonsense—for the moment—with a lash from a whip across the girl's shoulders.

He should never have done that, of course. Her eyes blaze for only a moment, but the damage is done. From then on she is not only wholeheartedly sympathetic towards Bond, who is just an attractive stranger, but she is antipathetic towards Mr. Big, who has been feeding her and clothing her since he picked her out of the gutter.

In due course, Bond inevitably escapes from the gangster. He is also instrumental in helping Solitaire to get away, and they leave New York together and speed south towards the town of St. Petersburg in cosy surroundings on a train. Ensconced in a Pullman compartment and passing themselves off as man and wife, with a long journey ahead of them, conditions couldn't be better for amorous dalliance, on the face of things. But Bond is still on a job, remember. Mr. Big's spies are everywhere: at Pennsylvania Station where they started from, on the train itself, and everywhere down the line to their destination.

It's a time for Bond to keep his eyes open, to exercise continued vigilance and not get caught with his trousers down—both figuratively and literally. But he can't completely resist an attractive woman, particularly one as forthcoming as Solitaire. Despite a broken finger—a little memento from his brush with the gangster—which is giving him much pain, Bond holds her in his good arm and kisses her. Then she takes over. 'She took his face between her two hands and held it away, panting. Her eyes were bright and hot. Then she brought his lips against hers again and kissed him long and lasciviously, as if she was the man and he the woman.' For an inexperienced girl, Solitaire is not doing badly. Perhaps she is just doing what comes naturally.

Bond would like to make love to her properly, but he can't, it seems, because of the broken little finger of his left hand. Anyway, it's too dangerous at the moment and they've got to get some sleep.

Solitaire sees the sense of this, but it doesn't prevent her from titillating Bond's feelings in a manner in which even an untutored virgin needs no instruction. He retires to the room next door while she undresses and prepares for bed. On his return the compartment smells of Balmain's 'Vent Vert' and Solitaire has climbed into the upper berth. After all, he's got a broken finger, and too much climbing about wouldn't be wise. In any case, it's better that he should take the lower berth in case of any trouble in the night. The girl is propped up with the bedclothes pulled up high. It's obvious that she's naked underneath them, and she makes a tantalizing vision. The moment he climbs towards her, presumably only to kiss her goodnight, she reaches out to him and the bedclothes drop away.

All Bond's resolutions nearly fly out of the window. Solitaire's explanation is a reasonable one, perhaps. 'It is fun for me to be able to tease such a strong silent man. You burn with such an angry flame. It is the only game I have to play with you and I shan't be able to play it for long.'

After a goodnight kiss more stimulating than soporific, she drops back on to the bed to sleep and tells him to get well quickly. 'I'm tired of my game already.'

They endure much dangerous and exciting adventure, both together and apart, during the ensuing pages, and there is very little time for love. They get caught again by Mr. Big, who has thought up something nice for them in the way of punishment. By this time the scene has shifted, and they are all on a ship in Jamaican waters. Mr. Big's penalty, to Bond for daring to oppose him and for killing several of his best men and to Solitaire for her treachery, is to tie them together and drag them through a shark-infested sea until they are eaten alive. Solitaire is stripped naked and she and Bond are tied together face to face.

'I didn't want it to be like this,' she tells him rather apologetically.

They survive this harrowing experience, but only at the expense of many painful if minor wounds. They are saved from drowning by a coral reef which, in Mr. Big's diabolical plan, had been enlisted to flay them. As a fleet of canoes skim out to their rescue, 'the first tears since his childhood' come into Bond's eyes and run 'down his drawn cheeks into the bloodstained sea.

Only a year previously, surely, his eyes had been wet on discovering Vesper's suicide?

After this adventure is over and the mission more or less completed, M sends him a message from London and grants him a fortnight's 'passionate leave'. Bond can't believe that his humourless and virtuous chief really dictated that word and assumes that he meant 'compassionate'.

By this time, of course, any pain or discomfort Bond might normally have felt from that broken finger is now forgotten. There are other wounds preventing him from making immediate love to Solitaire, for he is 'raw and bleeding in a hundred places' and a barracuda has taken a great chunk out of his shoulder. The girl is also pretty badly cut about, but it's nothing disfiguring or serious. But the book ends on a note of great promise. We may be sure that James Bond and Solitaire made good use of that 'passionate leave'.

We are halfway through the next adventure, *Moonraker* (1955), before the girl in the case puts in an appearance. Up to this point the narrative has been so absorbing that the lack of feminine interest has hardly been noticed. Paradoxically, there is the minimum of fireworks and derring-do in the early part of this book, and yet possibly paradox doesn't come into the matter at all. I'm almost inclined to believe that Ian Fleming could paraphrase the telephone directory and still be readable. But the fact of the matter is that although Bond is well in evidence he is not really on a case at all at this stage.

He is between assignments—always a dull time from *his* point of view—and he is pretty bored with things until M calls him in one day. It seems there's a little job James could do for the old man in a sort of personal capacity. M hums and hahs a bit before coming to the point. He's a stickler for rules and doesn't like the idea of employing Government personnel on private jobs. Still . . .

M is a member of Blade's, a gambling club in the St.

James' area with a great tradition. Sir Hugo Drax, a millionaire member who is personally financing a British guided missile he calls the Moonraker, is suspected of cheating at cards. The idea in M's mind is that Bond should show Drax up. This the Secret Service agent does, in a descriptive chapter or two so well handled by Ian Fleming that everything was as absorbing to me, whose knowledge of card games stops at Snap, as it might have been to Ely Culbertson.

Fascinating as the book has been till now, it is here that the real business begins. The long arm of coincidence stretches out and scoops both Drax and Bond into an exploit which I know many of Fleming's readers prefer beyond all others. But it is the girl we are concerned with for the time being.

Gala Brand is a policewoman, doing undercover work for the Special Branch. Not that Scotland Yard has any concrete reason to suspect that everything down at Drax's rocket site isn't all above board, but you can't be too careful where projects like this are concerned. She has been planted on Drax as his private secretary, but it looks like a routine job and she has never had anything to report. Then a German scientist shoots an Air Ministry security officer and kills himself, right on the job. It is done in a fit of jealousy: he claimed he was in love with Gala but had made no headway. He had blamed the security man for this, a man who is an entirely innocent pawn in the story but whose untimely demise gets Bond into the narrative as his replacement.

Gala is a heroine in the true Fleming tradition. When Bond first meets her he is impressed. 'Another Loelia Ponsonby. Reserved, efficient, loyal, virginal. Thank heavens, he thought. A professional.' *She* knows who he is, of course, just as *he* knows who she is really working for, but although they are in cohorts, she is deliberately remaining aloof. Bond is irritated at this, because he finds her attractive. Now, it should not be imagined that I suggest that Gala is in the Fleming tradition because she resembles Loelia. I am thinking, rather, of the stock requisites imbued in the less domestic female characters in the books. Gala has the physical attributes that seem to have been invested in Vesper and Solitaire, like a good figure, blue eyes and dark hair, and there appear to be very few of the fripperies and gew-gaws about her that Fleming obviously dislikes. She has no jewellery apart from a cameo brooch and a ring on her engagement finger. Additionally, except for 'the warm rouge on her lips, she wore no make-up and her nails were square cut with a natural polish.'

Cold and distant though she tries to be, Bond is warmed by one comforting thought. He has seen her dossier, and he knows that she has a mole on her breast. Somehow, that's reassuring.

It takes a bit of time for Bond's natural charm to break down her reserve a little, but he accomplishes it. They manage to get away from the plant for a bit, one glorious day. The Moonraker is sited not far from Dover, and they go walking along the beach, towards St. Margaret's Bay. It's lovely weather for a bathe, although they haven't come prepared. But since nobody is about Bond strips to his shorts and Gala, after a token argument which lasts about two lines, undresses to practically transparent nylon panties and brassière. During their bathe, Bond snatches a kiss, and the shock of it annoys her. 'These Secret Service people always seemed to have time for sex however important their jobs might be.' She snubs him for a little, although she does feel a bit ridiculous.

Later, all forgiven, they lie side by side under the cliff, to dry. The situation is idyllic, and there is no knowing what might have happened on that occasion had not someone dynamited the cliff above them in an attempt at murder. Bond manages to throw himself on top of Gala before they are covered by rocks and chalk dust, and since they are so close to the cliff itself their lives are saved. But getting free from the debris is quite an effort, and the remains of their shredded underclothing are completely torn off. Then they walk naked together into the sea to wash off the chalk and the dust. By this time, quite naturally, any modesty Gala might originally have felt is completely gone.

This narrow squeak and the fact that Bond has saved her life thaws Gala out more than a little. But there is no nonsense there under the cliff, despite their nakedness. James Bond, for one, doesn't feel any too armorous just at that moment. It's obvious now that someone back at Drax's plant doesn't like him, and his mind is almost a hundred per cent back on the job.

The pace of the story now begins to quicken, and neither he nor Gala have much time to think about anything but the work they have to do. Gala discovers that Drax's real plan with the rocket is nefarious, to say the least, and she is horrified. Drax tumbles that she's on to him and things look pretty bad for her for a time. Then Bond gets smashed up in a car on the Dover Road, and *his* future doesn't appear too rosy, either.

With the pair of them captured, and trussed up too, the outcome looks decidedly bleak. But Bond extricates them from their immediate discomfort in a manner which would not have disgraced Houdini. With his lips and teeth alone, more or less, he ignites a desk lighter—Ronson, of course—after having prepared a blowlamp—make not specified—and then, still with his mouth, lights the lamp. He doesn't accomplish this without a minor burn or two, yet the hard part is still to come. Holding the blowlamp between his teeth, Bond makes a superhuman effort to burn through the copper strands which immobilize Gala.

> He thought his jaw would break with the weight of the thing and the nerves of his front teeth screamed at him, but he swayed his chair carefully upright away from the desk and then strained his bent neck forward until the tip of blue fire from the torch was biting into the flex that bound Gala's right wrist to the arm of her chair.

He does it. And within a matter of seconds the girl has completely freed herself and untied him too.

Bond is a bit shaken by his endeavour and he quite understandably relaxes for a moment or two in order to recover, but 'he suddenly, delightedly felt Gala's soft lips on his mouth.' I imagine that even the amorous Bond thinks that there is a time and place for everything, but if the thought crossed his mind at that moment it didn't stay very long. The heat of the flame on Gala's wrists and forearms hasn't kindled a similar one in her breasts and loins. Although her eyes are shining, the kiss is sheer gratitude. ' "That's for what you did," she said seriously.'

Later, trapped together in a ventilator shaft, they get a steam hose turned on them. Knowing that this is going to happen, and in order to protect the girl as much as he possibly can, Bond wraps himself around her in a position which, under almost any other circumstances, might be described as compromising. She is a bit annoyed with him for thinking that she might consider her situation unmaidenly, but there is still enough of the prude in her to make a silent protest when he appears to be, on the face of things, trying 'a new position', so to speak. Silly bitch: he's only trying to save their lives. 'She squirmed furiously. "Don't be a bloody fool," whispered Bond, pulling her head close to his chest so that it was half covered by his open shirt.' That's telling her.

They weather this hazard, too. After it is all over, and Britain has been saved by the Secret Service once again, James Bond, together with all those reading about him, understandably expects great things. He has an appointment with Gala, and on his way to it he allows himself the luxury of visualizing the weeks ahead. He has planned a jaunt with the girl through France and Italy. He is so sure of himself that he has already arranged for a car to be at Calais by the following morning.

But for once Bond's romantic arrangements go awry. There is Another. We only get a glimpse of him, and then it's only a back view. He is a young detective-inspector with fair hair, trimmed short, and he is a hundred yards away. Gala is going to marry him, the very next afternoon. Remember that engagement ring on her finger? Her intended is a very dim figure, and he sounds rather dull. Still, there you are...

I think Gala Brand never knew what she missed.

By the time we meet James Bond again, in *Diamonds are Forever* (1956), he has forgotten all about that young lady—if he ever gave her another thought after the Moonraker case had been finally closed. As Gala had told him, there were plenty of other roses waiting to be picked.

His new adventure starts with M detailing him to break up a diamond-smuggling gang. By a fortunate chance Bond looks enough like the chap who has been employed to do the carrying to deceive anyone who has only heard the man described. So Scotland Yard nabs the crook just before he is due to report on the job and Bond takes over his name and his identity. The beauty of this little scheme is that nobody he will be encountering has ever met the carrier before. So Bond is on the inside and part of the pipeline almost from the start.

The first member of the gang he meets is Tiffany Case, to whom he reports for instructions at her hotel room in London. She is a small-time crook and an alcoholic, but Bond takes a fancy to her right away, and for good reason.

> She was sitting, half-naked, astride a chair in front of the dressing-table, gazing across the back of the chair into the triple mirror. Her bare arms were folded along the tall back of the chair and her chin was resting on her arms. Her spine was arched, and there was arrogance in the set of her head and shoulders. The black string of her brassière across the naked back, the tight black lace pants and the splay of her legs whipped at Bond's senses.

She is a blonde, with hair 'that fell heavily to the base of her neck'. Fleming, whom I suspect of possibly having swotted up a bit on diamonds before attempting to write about them, and quite righly too, tells us that the girl's eyes have chatoyance. This means that they seem to change colour, as the colour in the lustre of a jewel will change when it is moved in the light. Tiffany's eyes appear to 'vary between a light grey and a deep grey-blue.'

Her skin is tanned slightly, as with most good Fleming heroines, and naturally she doesn't wear make-up, except for deep red lipstick. Modesty does not appear to be one of her virtues, judging from her attire when she first meets Bond, for she makes no attempt to cover her semi-nakedness. She just carries on for a bit listening to a record, the music of which has 'her brazen sexiness, the rough tang of her manner and the poignancy...in her eyes.' She is quite a smart dresser when she gets around to putting something on, and her expensive-looking crocodile shoes have square toes.

Tiffany doesn't warm immediately to Bond, exactly, as Vesper did, and she doesn't start giving him the eye in the way that Solitaire did the moment she saw him. But she doesn't proffer the iceberg treatment like Gala, either. She just accepts him as being one of the gang, albeit a rather lowly and unfledged member, but she is affable enough in a somewhat hard-boiled and moody manner. She is dry and laconic as she gives him his instructions and she appears capable and businesslike. But she knows he's there all right, as a man as well as an accomplice, 'and there was an ironical tilt to the finely drawn eyebrows above the wide, level, rather scornful grey eyes that seemed to say, "Sure. Come and try. But brother, you'd better be tops."'

Despite this attitude she seems to be trying so hard to strike, the moment Bond gets a bit sociable and suggests that they might meet for dinner in New York after the job on hand is over Tiffany almost goes to pieces. She stammers, she turns away, and she agrees. But she doesn't look him in the eyes.

In brief, she is a true Fleming weirdie, but as far as I am concerned she is none the less real and captivating for that.

Arrived in New York, after having smuggled some diamonds across in a plane, one of the first people Bond runs into his his old pal Felix Leiter, who had helped him out in *Casino Royale* and *Live and Let Die*. Felix is now a Private Eye, working for Pinkerton's, and he seems to know quite a lot about Tiffany, so he gives Bond a brief biography. The girl has led a very varied life, doing all sorts of jobs from hat-check girl to lady's companion. She is also a backsliding member of 'Alcoholics Anonymous'. Her mother had run 'the snazziest cat-house in San Francisco,' but had rebelled against paying protection money to the local gang. The upshot of this was a visit from the whole mob, who ignored the girls who were there for the specific purpose 'but had themselves a gang-bang with Tiffany. She was only sixteen at the time.

Not surprising she won't have anything to do with men since then.' This information explains a lot.

'I'm not going to sleep with you,' Tiffany tells Bond just after they have had their first drink, preparatory to ordering dinner at that meeting they had agreed upon at the start of the operation. Nobody has even mentioned such a thing at this point, although if we know our man the idea has certainly crossed his mind. Despite Tiffany's defensive attitude, she is not above a little coquetry, and she asks Bond to say nice things about her dress or something. His reply betrays the fact that both he and Fleming like and dislike some of the same things.

'I love black velvet,' he tells her, 'especially against a sunburnt skin, and I'm glad you don't wear too much jewellery, and I'm glad you don't paint your fingernails.'

She doesn't reply to this, orally, but Bond has obviously said the right thing. She takes a slow drink, selects a cigarette and leans 'towards the flame of Bond's lighter. The valley between her breasts opened for him.' Things look decidedly promising, for although she still doesn't say anything with her mouth her eyes tell him quite a lot. ' "I like you," they said. "All is possible between us. But don't be impatient. And be kind. I don't want to be hurt any more." '

Their meal progresses, more or less conventionally, but Bond manages to pick up quite a little information about the gang he is after. This, when all is said and done, is really what he's there for. When Tiffany starts to get ever so slightly maudlin-tight—remember she's a lush—Bond decides to call it a day.

Tiffany Case is the original, crazy, mixed-up kid. From then on to the end of the chapter she vacillates like a metronome. After having spent quite a cosy evening together, while they drive together to her hotel in a taxi she keeps well away from Bond and she turns her back to him when he pays the driver. Bond notices that the knuckles of her hand are white when they go up in the elevator, but that could mean anything, either way, admittedly. But she doesn't try to stop him when he walks with her to her room. At the door she turns to him angrily, but there are tears in her eyes. Then suddenly he is in her embrace and she is telling him to look after himself. 'And then she pulled his face against hers and kissed him once, hard and long on the lips, with a fierce tenderness that was almost without sex.' But the moment Bond puts his arms round *her* she is out of his grasp and those eyes have the sultry glow. ' "Now get away from me," she said fiercely, and slammed the door and locked it.'

We don't get a lot more of Tiffany Case for a long time,

but when we do the locale has changed. We are whisked from New York to Las Vegas, and Bond, in his customary way, is headed straight for trouble. By the time he has been tumbled by the gang as 'a private eye of some sort' and has been almost kicked to death with football boots the girl is still vacillating, but in a different direction. She is now a renegade from the smuggling mob she works for and is well and truly on Bond's side. In fact, she is instrumental in helping them both to make a getaway.

Roaring on their way from Los Angeles to New York on a Constellation, 'Bond knew that he was very near to being in love with her.' Naturally, he knows, too, that if matters do reach a head between them there might be repercussions. 'Once he had taken her by the hand it would be for ever. He would be in the role of the healer, the analyst, to whom the patient had transferred her love and trust on her way out of her illness. There would be no cruelty equal to dropping her hand once he had taken it in his.'

Bond is in a dodgy position, but still, as Felix Leiter had told them just before he left them, 'Nothing propinks like propinquity.'

Things get a lot cosier once they are free from the American shore and are ploughing across the Atlantic on the *Queen Elizabeth*. They tell quite a lot about each other. Obviously, Tiffany has never run up against a man like this one in the whole of her sordid sojournings. I suppose it is inevitable that before long she wants to know the sort of girl Bond thinks would suit him as a soul mate. (Personal question?) Gallant as ever, he gives Tiffany a fair description of herself. Still, there is an element of sincerity about it.

'And you'd marry this person if you found her?'
'Not necessarily,' said Bond. 'Matter of fact I'm almost married already. To a man. Name begins with M. I'd have to divorce him before I tried marrying a woman. And I'm not sure I'd want that.'

Phew!—as they say. *We* know what he's on about, but remember that Tiffany knows very little about his job or background, even at this stage. What a stroke to come out with! Still, she must sense some underlying meaning in what he says, for she doesn't turn a hair. She doesn't pursue the matter, either. They talk about other things. Bond admits he'd like to have children. 'But only when I retire. Not fair on the children otherwise. My job's not all that secure.' The conversation isn't comfortable: Bond gives her the ball. Tiffany guesses that 'every girl would like to come home and find a hat on the hall table,' and she goes on to quote the chorines of Broadway: 'It's a lonesome wash without a man's shirt in it'.

To me, this sort of talk doesn't ring true. I have always been a trifle cynical about the idea of the domesticated showgirl, popularized in Hollywood, and also, in passing, by the golden-hearted whore, exemplified in the whimsicalities of Steinbeck. But perhaps I've led a sheltered life.

This isn't a mere digression. Possibly Tiffany isn't codding Bond along. I don't know: I'm stumped. They chat a bit more, and whether it's to mean wedding bells or not in the end, Tiffany finally succumbs. Their propinquity propinks, and she is a normal girl.

Taking her below to her cabin for the occupational therapy, Bond gets pulled along the corridor to his own cabin. 'I want it to be in your house, James.' And once in *his* house we see the Tiffany Case we knew was really there all the time.

> And after a while his other hand went to the zip fastener at the back of her dress and without moving away from him she stepped out of her dress and panted between their kisses. 'I want it all, James. Everything you've ever done to a girl. Now. Quickly.'
>
> And Bond bent down and put an arm round her thighs and picked her up and laid her gently on the floor.

I can't imagine why he chooses the floor with a perfectly good luxury liner bed an arm's length away, but I've no doubt at all that he knows what he's doing. After all, Bond has had enough experience in this gentle art.

I suppose all James Bond addicts have a favourite Fleming book and all of them have their favourite heroine, too. Mine can be found between the same covers: those of *From Russia, With Love* (1957). This is despite the fact that Bond does not show up until almost the first hundred pages have been read. But those hundred pages are so absorbing that you hardly notice his absence. For one thing, part of the time has been spent in the company of Tatiana Romanova.

She's quite a beauty. She looks rather like a young Greta Garbo, and she wears her hair in the way we will always associate with that fabulous star: it is 'brushed straight back from a tall brow and falling heavily down almost to the shoulders, there to curl up slightly at the ends.' Tatiana also has very deep blue eyes and long lashes.

His Women

Her figure is tall and graceful, and she is something of an athlete. Fleming tells us that a purist would have disapproved of her behind—well, I would certainly never have called myself a purist, but I must agree that her bottom doesn't seem very girlish. 'Its muscles were so hardened with exercise that it had lost the smooth downward feminine sweep, and now, round at the back and flat and hard at the sides, it jutted like a man's.'

Tatiana is still very attractive, even with that rump. But there is nothing particularly sophisticated about her. She has very simple tastes and she is easily pleased—probably because the poor girl has never known anything better. When we first meet her she is sitting in her one room in Moscow and thinking that she is happier than she has ever been before.

It doesn't seem to me that she has very much to be happy about. For a start, her room is 'a tiny box' in an enormous building which is the barracks of the State Security Department. Next, she has to share bathroom and lavatory with other girls. She *has* got a telephone and h. and c. but only one electric light. Still, in a room that size perhaps she wouldn't need any more. Further, her supper, which is cooking on the stove, consists of a pot of thick soup with a chunk of meat in it and some powdered mushroom. She thinks this is a bit of all right. She has a piece of black bread to go with it, too.

Tatiana has to wear a uniform, which tends to frighten off most people, so she is confined to the society of other employees in the M.G.B., the ministry for which she works. Her hours are from eight to six, and she does Saturday mornings as well, it seems—or their Russian equivalent—and she doesn't get a full hour for lunch. 'But it was a good lunch, a real meal, and you could do with little supper and save up for the sable coat that would one day take the place of the well-worn Siberian fox.'

Poor Tatiana. Her life looks a pretty grim one, and she hasn't got a lot to look forward to. Promotion from Corporal, her present rank, to Colonel seems a long grind, and in the end a three-room flat with bathroom, six floors above her present box, appears to be the best thing she can anticipate. It doesn't look as if she will ever get that far, since she's so pretty that the general opinion is that very soon one of the high-ranking officers is going to elevate her to the position of wife or mistress. She won't have much say in the matter.

Whatever *she* thinks about it I would say that an M.G.B. girl's lot is not a happy one. But she is enjoying it when she receives a peremptory telephone call which jerks her out of her fool's paradise and into a James Bond adventure.

SMERSH is cooking up a *konspiratsia*. Bond has got to go, and he must be killed with ignominy. The plan is quite an involved one. The man who devises it informs SMERSH that it will 'require a reliable and extremely beautiful girl.'

Tatiana is to be the bait, naturally. The idea is that she is to pretend that she has fallen in love with Bond from photos and a file she has been working on. She is to give the impression that she wishes to defect from the Soviet Union to Britain, and for this privilege she is willing to bring over with her a much-coveted cipher machine. The only condition is that Bond must go out and get it—and her—in Istanbul.

M and the Secret Service aren't exactly mugs. They know it's a trap of some sort, but it's necessary to play along as far as possible in order to find out what's what. M had been a bit diffident about things before trying to sell Bond the idea of getting into this affair. After all, he'd heard things. There was some talk of Bond marrying Tiffany Case.

But it's all right. That's all over. Tiffany had met a fellow in the American Embassy and intended to marry *him*. 'They've both gone back to the States, as a matter of fact. Probably better that way... nice enough fellow. Probably suit her better than living in London... Fine girl, but she's a bit neurotic... Anyway it's over now.' Phew! After all that business about there being no cruelty equal to dropping her hand once he had taken it in his he'd had me worried. But it looks as though if any dropping of hands was done Tiffany did it. So, in brief, Bond is still a free agent and he can play along with this fishy-looking affair that has just turned up from Turkey.

James Bond's first sight of most of his girl friends has been under more or less conventional circumstances—up to this point in the saga, at least. But his introduction to Tatiana, and hers to him, is most unconventional. He has actually *seen* her before, but only through a periscope, and at a distance. Now he is in his hotel room in Istanbul. He has had a hard and tiring day and she is not in his mind at all at the moment. It is late at night, and he has just had a shower. He is quite naked. Suddenly, as he bends to turn off the light, a voice speaks out of the shadows. 'Poor Mr. Bond. You must be tired. Come to bed.'

Now, this sort of situation is of the kind which any dreamer worthy of the name has at some time or another incorporated into his fantasies. He has also rejected such pipe-dreams as being unworthy of him, if only because they are altogether too unlikely. Yet the unlikely thing about this particular situation, to me, is not that here is a girl waiting in

His Women

the bed for Bond but that the girl should be the modest and unsophisticated Tatiana.

SMERSH has coached her well, for her brazen act fools the reader as well as it fools James Bond. She might have been doing this sort of thing for years, and there is no doubt that she is enjoying it. She teases him like an accomplished coquette. All she's wearing under the single sheet is a thin black ribbon round her neck and black silk stockings rolled to her knees. He is not so daft that it doesn't cross his mind that there might be something phoney about the whole business: this is too good to be true. But still, she *had* claimed that she was in love with him, and she *has* brought the cipher machine, and she *did* want to get away as soon as possible.

Poor old Bond. 'God, he thought. I hope it's all right. I hope this crazy plan will work. Is this wonderful girl a cheat? Is she true? Is she real?' He soon finds out. Tatiana's 'hand came up round his neck and pulled him fiercely down to her. At first the mouth trembled under his and then, as passion took her, the mouth yielded into a kiss without end.'

What neither of them know is that the ornate mirror over the bed-head is a false one, and that a couple of SMERSH men are behind it filming their antics.

> And the view-finders gazed coldly down on the passionate arabesques the two bodies formed and broke and formed again, and the clockwork mechanism of the cine-cameras whirred softly on as the breath rasped out of the open mouths of the two men and the sweat of excitement trickled down their bulging faces into their cheap collars.

The scene they are watching and filming had started 'from the shadows at the back of the room.' Bond did turn on 'the pink-shaded light by the bed' when he came over to Tania, but what is its wattage? 60? 100? 150? Pretty dim, and it's shaded, too. Those cameramen must have been using an amazingly fast film. The false mirror would act as a neutral density filter, too. It wouldn't exactly help matters. I suppose the thing *could* be done, with very special equipment. But my exposure meter won't give me a reading at *any* speed under similar conditions. I've tried it. Of course, I didn't have a Tatiana there. Perhaps her skin gave off a glow bright enough to film by? I can almost believe it.

We are next treated to one of those stirring train rides which Ian Fleming describes so well and on which so many exciting things happen to Bond. On this occasion it's aboard the Orient Express, which runs from Istanbul to Paris. Bond and Tatiana are posing as man and wife, as he and Solitaire did on a train in the States a few years earlier. But this time Bond hasn't got a broken finger.

He *has* got enemies on the train, but he's also got allies, too. These enable him to spend plenty of time alone with Tatiana, and it must not be forgotten that she has already had a taste of his prowess.

The train has hardly started before the beautiful Russian girl starts too. They are still moving through the outskirts of Istanbul when she 'moved her knee so that it touched him.' A few thoughts of the night before encourage her further. 'He read her eyes. He bent and put his hands on the fur over her breasts and kissed her hard on the lips. Tatiana leant back, dragging him with her.'

But there are interrupted. Darko Kerim, an ally, has noticed three M.G.B. men on the train, and it looks like a double-cross on Tatiana's part. But Bond trusts her—who wouldn't?—although things now look so dangerous that he must keep his eyes open all the time in the immediate future. There can be no sleep for him now—much less love-making. It's all right for the girl to sleep, although she insists on being in his arms. 'She had taken off all her clothes, except the black ribbon round her throat, and had pretended not to be provocative as she scrambled impudicitly into bed and wriggled herself into a comfortable position.' The little tease.

Things move fast in this particular book. Bond has so much to do on that train journey that the romantic content suffers. Between other exciting happenings, however, he does eventually manage to get a bit of sleep.

It was dusk when Bond awoke in the soft cradle of her lap. At once, as if she had been waiting for the moment, Tatiana took his face between her hands and looked down into his eyes and said urgently, '*Dushka*, how long shall we have this for?'

'For long.' Bond's thoughts were still luxurious with sleep.

'But for how long?'

He knows it can't be for very long. After all, she *is* an enemy agent, although she has really fallen for him now, and he for her. She has spilled the beans about the *konspiratsia*, and has had nagging doubts about SMERSH's concern for her. Bond has no illusions at all. He can see her future. The best she can expect is a new name, a new life in Canada, perhaps,

His Women

and a thousand pounds a year. He lets the girl down as lightly as he can.

> 'As long as possible. It will depend on us. Many people will interfere. We shall be separated. It will not always be like this in a little room. In a few days we shall have to step out into the world. It will not be easy. It would be foolish to tell you anything else.'

What *did* exactly happen to Tania, I wonder, eventually? Much happens to James Bond, we know, before this book is over. We also know that he sees her safe and sound in the Embassy in Paris. But there is no erotic fade-out *this* time. Far from it. I like to think that somewhere in the western world Tania is sitting in a pleasant room, just as happy with her present lot as she was in that tiny room in Moscow. Perhaps she is waiting for a word from her James, and hoping that one day they will meet again. It's just possible. After all, Felix Leiter is always popping up in Bond's life, and some of the other characters return in later books. Why not Tatiana Romanova? I, for one, could stand it.

They are fortuitous circumstances, perhaps, and also extremely fortunate ones that James Bond should, more and more as often as not get his first sight of his lady loves when they are in a state of near-nudity. It hadn't always been like this, but after *Moonraker* he hit a winning streak. Tiffany Case was in a black brassière and panties. Tatiana Romanova, when he first got a close glimpse of her, was clothed in less: a black neck-band and stockings up to her knees. But Honeychile Rider, when he first sees that engaging nymph in *Dr. No* (1958), is wearing even less that that!

Bond is on the beach of a private island near Jamaica at the time, and he is investigating the behaviour and pursuits of a suspicious Chinese doctor who gives that book its name. He is trespassing, and on dangerous ground, so that even though he has just woken up somewhat lazily he is still pretty sharp when a shadow across the sand attracts his attention. It is no wonder that what he sees makes his heart miss a beat and then start pounding, with his eyes 'fierce slits.' I think the occasion justifies Ian Fleming's full description.

> It was a naked girl, with her back to him. She was not quite naked. She wore a broad leather belt around her waist with a hunting knife in a leather sheath at her right hip. The belt made her nakedness extraordinarily

erotic. She stood not more than five yards away on the tideline looking down at something in her hand. She stood in the classical relaxed pose of the nude, all the weight on the right leg and the left knee bent and turning slightly inwards, the head to one side as she examined the things in her hand.

It was a beautiful back. The skin was a very light uniform *café au lait* with the sheen of dull satin. The gentle curve of the backbone was deeply indented, suggesting more powerful muscles than is usual in a woman, and the behind was almost as firm and rounded as a boy's. The legs were straight and beautiful and no pinkness showed under the slightly lifted left heel. She was not a coloured girl.

No, she is an ash blonde, and her hair comes down to her shoulders. When Bond lets her know that he is there and watching her she doesn't 'cover her body with the two classical gestures.' One hand does go down to her loins but the other goes up to her face. She has good reason for this instinctive movement. 'It was a beautiful face, with wide-apart deep blue eyes under lashes paled by the sun ... It was ... the face of a girl who fends for herself. And once, reflected Bond, she had failed to fend. For the nose was badly broken, smashed crooked like a boxer's.'

Honey, as she is called, is a child of nature. In fact, she's almost infantile in some ways. This isn't surprising, I suppose, because she has had a very strange upbringing—if you could call it that. When she was five her mother and father had been killed when their Jamaican house burned down. She has lived in the cellars of the ruins ever since; with her black nanny until she was fifteen and on her own from then till now. She is twenty. One of the few things salvaged from the fire was an encyclopedia. Having started to read it at the age of eight, from the letter A, she is gradually working her way right through it. This makes her, if not exactly a well-educated young lady, at least one with all sorts of out of the way scraps of knowledge.

Since she has lived alone for so long, Honey doesn't trust humans a lot but she gets on very well with reptiles and animals, as lots of them periodically migrate to her abode for shelter when the cane is being cut. She refers to them as people and thinks of them as such. Her misanthropy, under the circumstances, is quite understandable, particularly since she appears to have been fair game to the lechers in the district, one of whom eventually caught her, smashed her in the face and broke her nose and then raped her while she was unconscious. Her revenge for this was to creep up to his

His Women

house one dark night and empty a Black Widow spider out of a box on to the man's stomach. She is quite happy at the recollection. It hurt him quite a lot and he didn't die for a week.

She lives by collecting the sea-shells and selling them to an American dealer. She learned that they were saleable from the encyclopedia, and she seems to be making a fair living at it. Her idea is to save enough money to go to the States and have an operation on her nose. She is very naïve, for her ambition when her nose is straightened is to be a call girl, a career which looks pretty rewarding from her point of view, and which she explains in detail to Bond.

> 'One of those girls who has a beautiful flat and lovely clothes. You know what I mean,' she said impatiently. 'People ring them up and come and make love to them and pay them for it. They get hundreds of dollars for each time in New York. That's where I thought I'd start. Of course,' she admitted, 'I might have to do it for less to begin with. Until I learned to do it really well. How much do you pay the untrained ones?'

By this time, what with all these confidences, Honey feels quite pally towards Bond. She is a trespasser on this island, too—after sea-shells—and she has heard all about the sinister Dr. No. Bond has given her his sleeping-bag for the night, and when it's time for bye-bye she feels so cosy towards her new-found friend that she generously invites him in, if he would like it. He'd like it, all right, but he's got to be on the *qui vive* and he declines the offer. Honey apparently thinks she might have given him the wrong impression, for 'If you're thinking ... I mean—you don't have to make love to me ... we could sleep back to front, you know, like spoons." (How naïve can one get?)

Although Bond admits that it would be nice he still won't do it. But she won't go to sleep until he promises to come in with her one day when they get back to Jamaica. He promises. 'Now you owe me slave-time. You've promised. Good night, darling James.'

It isn't very long after this that Dr. No captures the pair of them. Bond makes an effort to pass himself off as an ornithologist and Honey as his wife. 'Marrying' his girl of the moment when they are in a tight spot is one of his favourite gambits and a fairly regular attempt at subterfuge.

Their reception is right royal. Dr. No is a thoughtful and most generous captor. They are ensconced in a room which is nothing short of palatial, with all the luxuries to hand that one could think of. Under different circumstances their situation would be idyllic: even as things are it makes fascinating reading. Fleming calls the chapter 'Mink-Lined Prison.'

Honey wants a bath before settling down to eat, but she has never been in an ordinary bathroom before—'I don't know how to work one of those places'—much less the extraordinary one they have with all its modern gimmickry. She is so provocative that it is all Bond can do to keep his hands off her, so he goes and turns the water on for her while she undresses and puts on a kimono. It doesn't exactly help matters when he feels both of her arms go round his neck while he's testing the water.

> ... The golden body blazed in the white tiled bathroom. She kissed him hard and clumsily on the lips. He put his arms round her and crushed her to him, his heart pounding. She said breathlessly at his ear, 'The Chinese dress felt strange. Anyway, you told that woman we were married.'
>
> Bond's hand was on her left breast. Its peak was hard with passion. Her stomach pressed against his. Why not? Why not? Don't be a fool! This is a crazy time for it. You're both in deadly danger. You must stay cold as ice to have any chance of getting out of this mess. Later! Later! Don't be weak.

Bond just about has the strength to extricate himself from this predicament, but Honey isn't one to give up too easily. Once in the bath she wants him to wash her!

She teases him all through their meal, doing what comes naturally in the way of flirtation in a manner which makes the equally inexperienced Solitaire look like a prude in retrospect. I think Honey would have won and had her way with Bond had they been guests of any other personage than Dr. No. That diabolical gentleman had drugged their coffee, and the girl is fast asleep even before Bond. He just about makes it to his bed before passing out.

Their captor had known all about them, of course, right from the start. He hadn't been fooled for a minute: he was just playing with them. He intends to kill them, but not quickly and easily. In the matter of thinking up unpleasant deaths Dr. No and Mr. Big make a fine pair. Honey is to be stripped and tied down to the ground with pegs. The local black land crabs are on a compulsive migration, like lemmings, but they devour everything in their path, like locusts. The idea is to see how long the girl will last before she is eaten to death. It's all in the interest of science, really. Bond's fate is to be just as unpleasant, if rather more varied. Dr. No has constructed 'an obstacle race, an assault course against death.' He doesn't give any further details, because that would destroy the element of surprise for Bond. Again, the object of the exercise is to see how far the captive can get before being killed.

James Bond runs that frightening obstacle race in a very long but wonderful descriptive passage which finds him still whole but badly burned and bruised at the finish. It looks to him as if Honey is done for, but she survives, too. Her ordeal didn't turn out nearly as badly as might have been anticipated. The doctor wasn't to know that she got on better with crabs and suchlike than she did with people, and anyway she knew a lot more about them and their habits than he did. She just lay still. 'I got fond of them. They were company.' The hardest part of the whole thing was freeing herself from the pegs after the crabs had gone.

Away from the island, the villain's guns spiked, all reports sent to London, sick leave applied for, and the moping-up operations left to others, Bond and Honey finally get a little time to themselves with no danger hanging over them. She takes him to her home, which isn't nearly so much of a rathole as he had imagined it.

She gives him a nice cold dinner of lobster and fruit, but while he is eating she wants him to tell her everything he knows about love. What with her 'full red lips ... open with excitement and impatience' and 'the points of her breasts ... hard and roused' showing through the tight cotton blouse it's small wonder that James Bond's mouth gets dry and he can't eat any more. 'Honey, I can either eat or talk love to you. I can't do both.'

Well—you can always eat, can't you?

She undresses in the moonlight, starts to undress him, and then leads him to the bedroom. On the bed itself is a sleeping-bag she has just bought. 'It's a double one. It cost a lot of money. Take those off and come in. You promised. You owe me slave-time.'

The amazing thing about Bond, to me, is not his adroitness in casting off these randy lovelies, but that he should ever want to.

It is not easy to say exactly *who* is the heroine of *Goldfinger* (1959). There are two or three entries to choose from. The first one we meet is called Jill Masterson, and she is practically naked at the time. (Surprise, surprise?) A black brassière and black silk briefs is all she is wearing when both we and James Bond first get a glimpse of her. It is early on in the book and I think one may be forgiven for thinking that she is to be his popsy throughout it. She has all the physical attributes. 'She was very beautiful. She had the palest blonde hair. It fell heavily to her shoulders, unfashionably long. Her eyes were deep blue against a lightly sunburned skin and her mouth was bold and generous.' She is also tall, round about five feet ten, which makes her a big girl even for Fleming, who likes 'em long. She has good breasts, too, and they 'thrust against the black silk of the brassière.'

Only one thing about her is disquieting. 'She had just finished painting the nails of her left hand.' If I had been given overnight notice of the number of runners in this particular classic I think I would have scrubbed her as co-favourite and would have chalked her up at about six to four against on that information alone.

Still, heroine or not, Jill and Bond don't manage too badly together. They have a trip on a train, this time from Miami to New York, and something exciting always happens when our man climbs on to a train with a pretty girl. For once there is no shooting, and there isn't an enemy in sight to worry about.

> It had been a wonderful trip up in the train ... to the rhythm of the giant diesels pounding out the miles, they had made long, slow love in the narrow berth. It had been as if the girl was starved of physical love. She had woken him twice more in the night with soft demanding caresses, saying nothing, just reaching for his hard, lean body. The next day she had twice pulled down the roller blinds to shut out the hard light and had taken him by the hand and said, 'Love me, James' as if she was asking for a sweet.

She sounds like a nympho to me, but perhaps I am being less than just. After all, it wasn't *any* old Tom, Dick or Harry cooped up with her on this cosy journey. I suppose one should make allowances.

She definitely does look like the limpet type, though, but Bond frees himself from her in a manner which must have left her gasping. He had earned himself ten thousand dollars back in Miami just for doing a chap a favour, which had led him to meet Jill in the first place, and he makes her take the money. 'It ought to be a million,' he tells her.

Then he gives her one hard kiss and he's away. I imagine Jill Masterson standing on that platform with her head in a whirl, feeling like a tart who has been paid off. But I can't imagine that the size of the windfall had necessarily taken her breath away. She had been doing all right. Goldfinger employs her at a hundred pounds a week, and all found, and she is saving.

His Women

Whatever she is thinking and feeling at this moment—although neither she nor Bond 'had any regrets'—we know what is going on through *his* mind as he drives off in a taxi: 'Some love is fire, some love is rust. But the finest, cleanest love is lust.'

The next young lady to drop into Bond's life in *Goldfinger* calls herself Tilly Soames. It happens in France, some time later. Bond is driving an Aston Martin and he is trailing Goldfinger himself, who is in a Rolls. The pursuer keeps noticing a little Triumph, driven by girl, which is sometimes behind him and sometimes in front. It soon becomes obvious that she is not sticking close by sheer coincidence, but whatever her motives may be in the matter he feels it necessary to put her *hors de combat*. He jams on his brakes at a convenient moment and then quickly backs up. The inevitable collision does the Triumph more harm than it does the Aston Martin.

By the time Bond has alighted and gone round to assess the damage, Tilly has 'one beautiful silken leg on the road', and there is 'an indiscreet glimpse of white thigh.' Bond takes a look at the wreckage to the two cars, her particularly, and his opening gambit is: 'If you touch me there again you'll have to marry me.' For this he receives a stinging slap across the face.

He doesn't mind particularly. He has accomplished what he wanted to do and has put this girl's car out of action. He offers to pay for all the damage and to settle her hotel expenses for the night, but Tilly isn't interested. She is furious. She is also extremely anxious. She pleads an urgent appointment an asks to come with him.

Now Bond has a pretty important appointment, too. He's on a job and as I say, he's trailing Goldfinger who is a wrong 'un. But he sizes the girl up and then agrees to take her. It's always difficult for him to refuse a lovely girl.

Tilly certainly is attractive. She has blue eyes, for a start. Her fingernails, too, are not painted. More—as Dornford Yates used to say. 'Although she was a very beautiful girl she was the kind who leaves her beauty alone. She had made no attempt to pat her hair into place.'

She is now a firm favourite in the heroine stakes. Her clothes which are not particularly feminine, *have* got one or two Fleming preferences which save the day. She has a wide black stitched leather belt and she wears a pleated skirt. Although her white silk shirt is a bit mannish she is not too masculine, what with 'her fine breasts out-thrown and unashamed under the taut silk.'

But the time they reach Geneva, their destination, they

have got to know each other slightly, but she hasn't fallen under Bond's spell. She obviously has an urgent job on hand and she ditches him as soon as she can. It's strictly no nonsense with Tilly.

Bond's immediate task is to try and find out what is going on in a highly-suspicious factory of Goldfingers', and not very long afterwards, while he is studying the place from some trees in the grounds, he meets the girl again. She is spread-eagled under a tree, dressed entirely in black and with a rifle trained on the factory. She looks like messing up the whole operation. Since it is a desperate case it needs a desperate remedy. Bond makes a pancake landing on her back and induces brief unconsciousness with a slight pressure on her cartoid artery.

Later, when it has been fully established that they are both after the same man it transpires that Tilly is Jill Masterson's sister! And Goldfinger has killed Jill.

It seems that Goldfinger's habit is to ration himself to one woman a month. First he hypnotizes her, and then he paints her gold. He does this because by carnally possessing a golden girl he gets as near as he can to marrying the precious metal, which he loves above all else. He always leaves the backbones unpainted, so that the girls' bodies can 'breathe.' If he didn't do this they would die. He then gives them a thousand dollars each for their services and co-operation. As his revenge on Jill for going with Bond he had painted her all over.

Dying in a Miami hospital, Jill had had the savvy to cable Tilly and tell her all about it when she arrived, but why wasn't she bright enough to explain to the doctors or even to tell the police who was responsible? I suppose nobody could have pinned it on Goldfinger as a murder, though. He was too cunning and clever.

Tilly maintains considerable hostility towards Bond even after telling him this story and knowing that her sister had had a soft spot for him. One wonders how long it is going to be before she starts to melt. She is not even very keen about letting him take over the task of bringing Goldfinger to book, but she does finally agree to back him up. 'Only don't ever touch me or I shall kill you.'

They travel far and go through quite a lot together, but she remains hostile. Yet she looks to be the favourite still, even when Pussy Galore puts in an appearance. Pussy is the only woman in America who runs a gang. She used to be a trapeze artist, but her team of girls was so unsuccessful that she trained them as cat burglars instead. They are all Lesbians, and are so ruthless and accomplished that even the big male gangs now respect them.

Bond liked the look of her. He felt the sexual challenge all beautiful Lesbians have for men. He was amused by the uncompromising attitude that said to Goldfinger and the room, 'All men are bastards and cheats. Don't try any masculine hocus on me. I don't go for it. I'm in a separate league.' Bond thought she would be in her early thirties. She had pale, Rupert Brooke good looks with high cheek-bones and a beautiful jawline. She had the only violet eyes Bond had ever seen. They were the true deep violet of a pansy and they looked candidly out at the world from beneath straight black brows. Her hair, which was as black as Tilly Masterson's, was worn in an untidy urchin cut. The mouth was a decisive slash of deep vermilion. Bond thought she was superb and so, he noticed, did Tilly Masterson who was gazing at Miss Galore with worshipping eyes and lips that yearned. Bond decided that all was now clear to him about Tilly Masterson.

So another firm favourite turns out to be false. Pussy looks like an outsider, too.

Bond never gets a chance to really try his masculine charms on Tilly. At a crucial moment in the story, when he and the girl are making a getaway from the Goldfinger mob, her stubbornness and sexual inclinations cost her her life. 'The girl's hand tugged at him. She screamed angrily, "No. No. Stop! I want to stay close to Pussy. I'll be safe with her." ' She gets a broken neck from Goldfinger's henchman.

At this stage we are now rapidly approaching the end of the book and there isn't a heroine in sight. There are only a few pages to go and Bond is in his usual tight spot. This time he is high up above the clouds over the Atlantic in a B.O.A.C. plane, stolen by the Goldfinger gang and with quite a number of them on board too, Pussy included. On the face of things Bond hasn't got a hope in hell of extricating himself from this mess, but here Fleming plays his trump. Bond is slipped a small paper message, and the message says: 'I'm with you. XXX.P.' What a turn up for the book!

So with the totally unexpected help of an ally hitherto wholeheartedly in the enemy camp, Bond is enabled to crash the plane and save the day. He and the girl float in their life-jackets until a lifeboat gets to them. Everyone else goes to the bottom.

Later, lying comfortably in a warm cabin of a weathership, he is visited by Pussy from the cabin next door.

... She was wearing nothing but a grey fisherman's jersey that was decent by half an inch. The sleeves were rolled up. She looked like a painting by Vertes. She said, 'People keep asking me if I'd like an alcohol rub and I keep on saying that if anyone's going to rub me it's you, and if I'm going to be rubbed with anything it's you I'd like to be rubbed with.' She ended lamely, 'So here I am.'

She knows she is due for Sing Sing, but she is going to make the best of things before she goes. At Bond's command she takes off the sweater and gets into bed with him.

Bond looked down into the deep blue-violet eyes that were no longer hard, imperious. He bent and kissed them lightly. He said, 'They told me you only liked women.'

Well, she certainly fooled me. I thought so, too. But as she explains, 'I never met a man before.'

In 1960 Ian Fleming did not give us the usual yearly adventure. Instead, he offered us several: five secret occasions in the life of James Bond. These are to be found in a book of short stories with the over-all title of *For Your Eyes Only*.

One of the tales is not strictly an adventure at all, but the other four are, and they are naturally considerably briefer than the other yarns. A lot of readers did not like this new departure. I didn't mind it. For one thing, there are four times as many girls. They are a mixed bag. The first one we meet is, like Bond, a member of the Secret Service. He is in Paris at the time, sitting at a pavement café having a drink, when a battered old car shoots out of the traffic and pulls into the kerb in front of him. Out gets a girl.

... Bond sat up. She had everything, but absolutely everything that belonged in his fantasy. She was tall and, although her figure was hidden by a light raincoat, the way she moved and the way she held herself promised that it would be beautiful.

She has long blonde hair under a beret and her eyes are wide apart and blue. 'The pale skin was velvet. The blonde hair was silk—to the roots.' Mary Ann Russell is a veritable dish, and I am inclined to resent the fact that Fleming practically throws her away in a story which does not give him very much time to develop her. Come to think of it, she is hardly necessary to the tale at all. Put a young male Secret

Service man in her place and things would not be *very* much different. They might be duller, though. Still, Mary Ann *is* in the Service; it's always possible that Bond's path will cross hers again some day.

Mary Ann Russell has come to the café to find Bond. There is bad news back at the office and he's wanted. So off we go into another adventure, brief though it may be.

The Russians are up to their tricks again. This time they have killed a despatch rider near SHAPE headquarters and stolen important secret papers. Bond does a neat bit of detective work in discovering their camouflaged hideout in a clearing in a forest, and he spends a very long time lying flat, quite still, watching and waiting for something to happen. His only company are a couple of hedge-sparrows, who are building a nest.

When the *dénouement* comes, Bond is in a rather tough spot. It is in the clearing, and he is pretty sure he's had it this time. But it was a good thing that Mary Ann had come along, uninvited, and had brought a .22 target pistol with her.

I said that this story would not be *very* much different without her. I employed the italicized word advisedly. James Bond is grateful to Mary Ann for saving his life, and he shows her his gratitude in the best way he knows. 'Bond took the girl by the arm. He said: "Come over here. I want to show you a bird's nest." '

On reflection, I wonder if I was right in saying that she was hardly necessary?

In the next story, which takes its title from the book and is called 'For Your Eyes Only', Bond's mission is quite straightforward. It is a simple one of assassination. An elderly couple in Jamaica called Havelock have been cold-bloodedly murdered. M knows who did it: he's got contacts. The culprit is a former Gestapo man named von Hammerstein, who had wanted to get hold of the couple's property. M knows where he is hiding out, too, and it is right up in the north of the United States, near the Canadian border. There is nothing at all in the way of evidence to pin the double murder on to von Hammerstein, and in fact the case doesn't exactly come within M's province at all. But he had been best man at the Havelock's wedding, many years before. That makes things different. It is obviously a case for rough justice. Bond takes on the job of administering it.

His task is remarkably uncomplicated but extremely delicate. It is really a stalk: a sort of stealthy big-game hunt somewhat in the style of *Rogue Male*. The prize is the life of a man the law can't touch and the penalty, if Bond fails, or is caught, his own life.

By himself he would have walked it. But there are complications, naturally. A *girl* turns up, intent upon doing the same job as Bond, and with a *bow and arrow!*

> The girl looked like a beautiful unkempt dryad in ragged shirt and trousers. The shirt and trousers were olive green, crumpled and splashed with mud and stains and torn in places, and she had bound her pale blonde hair with goldenrod to conceal its brightness for her crawl through the meadow. The beauty of her face was wild and rather animal, with a wide sensuous mouth, high cheek-bones and silvery-grey disdainful eyes. There was the blood of scratches on her forearms and down one cheek, and a bruise had puffed and slightly blackened the same cheek-bone.

A most unglamorous heroine, this one, but none the less fetching for all that.

Her name is Judy Havelock—did you guess?—and she is here to avenge her murdered parents. But she is a little more amenable to sensible argument than was hot-headed Tilly, back in *Goldfinger*. She isn't a Lesbian either.

Judy gets shot, not fatally, but somewhat picturesquely, by a bullet which leaves a bruised, bleeding gash across the muscle of her arm. This is the next best thing to the 'just a scratch' sort of wound suffered by so many heroes and heroines in fiction. Bond washes the injury clean with coffee and whisky, then takes a thick slice of bread from his haversack and binds it up with his handkerchief, cut into three strips and joined together. While he is doing all this her mouth is very close. 'The scent of her body had a warm animal tang. Bond kissed her once softly on the lips and once again, hard. He tied the knot. He looked into the grey eyes close to his. They looked surprised and happy.' No wonder! Judy seems ready for surrender. 'She said docilely: "Where are you taking me?" ' He tells her. Their destination is London, via Canada, but first they will be staying in a place called the KO-ZEE Motel. She likes this: she's never stayed in a motel before. We are told little more, but I think we may safely assume that the adventure had a happy ending and that this episode may be counted as one of James Bond's successes.

The third girl to enter his life in this particular book is called Lisl Baum. I don't like her very much. She is referred to by one of the characters, and correctly, no doubt, as 'a luxus whore'. But this is not why I don't like her: I have no

His Women

antipathy towards whores, luxus or otherwise. She is certainly attractive enough for anybody. Bond noticed her right away. 'Every man in the restaurant would have noticed her. She had the gay, bold, forthcoming looks the Viennese are supposed to have and seldom do. There was a vivacity and charm about her that lit up her corner of the room. She had the widest possible urchin cut in ash blonde, a pert nose, a wide laughing mouth and a black ribbon round her throat.'

Quite apart from her looks she has a provocativeness that ought to be endearing. After she meets Bond she invites him to visit her a day or two later on a lonely beach. ' "I shall be getting my last sunburn before the winter. Among the sanddunes. You will see a pale yellow umbrella. Underneath it will be me." She smiled. "Knock on the umbrella and ask for Fraulein Lisl Baum." ' But when he gets there, Bond doesn't knock. Did you expect him to? 'The hands flew to the top scrap of the bikini and pulled it up... The bright shadow of the umbrella covered only her face. The rest of her—a burned cream body in a black bikini on a black and white striped bath-towel—lay offered to the sun.'

No, there is nothing wrong with that. She's not particularly hard to get, either. After the successful conclusion of his mission, Bond almost has her handed to him on a plate. Her boy friend gives him the key to her hotel room! He 'put his hand to his heart and looked seriously into Bond's eyes. "I give it to you from my heart. Perhaps also from hers." '

She is personable, she is sexy, and she is available: cardinal virtues in any woman, surely? Why, then, can't I like Lisl Baum? I think it must be her name, and I am rather sensitive to names. It is the one ugly thing about her. After Vesper Lynd, Simone Latrelle, Gala Brand, Tiffany Case, Tatiana Romanova, Honeychile Rider, the Masterson pair and Pussy Galore—*well*, wouldn't you tend to bracket Lisl Baum among the Rosa Klebbs and Irma Bunts?

The fourth and last charmer to appear in *For Your Eyes Only* ought to affect me in the same way. Her name is Liz Krest. In comparison with this the appellation of Lisl Baum almost trips off the lips and is music to the ears.

Strange as it may appear, I don't mind Liz, although she is a bit of a bitch, and is married to a *son*-of-a-bitch of the first water—if he ever drank any. I can only think that my predilection arises because first impressions are important, particularly in short stories. Ian Fleming introduced us to Lisl Baum by name before we ever know what she looked like. But we know what Liz looks like before we ever know her name. So does James Bond: '... a naked sunburned girl came down the steps into the saloon. No, she wasn't quite naked after all, but the pale brown satin strips of bikini were designed to make one think she was.' After that introduction one doesn't care *what* she is called.

But this may be over-simplification. While I admit that I was attracted to Mary Ann Russell, Judy Havelock and Liz Krest *before* I knew their names, and did not like Lisl Baum, whatever she looked like, because I did know hers, I do not necessarily admit that things need have stayed that way. Ian Fleming is the phenomenon he is, in my opinion, primarily because of his subtle character-drawing. We are carried along in his books because we believe in his people, no matter what outlandish tricks they may get up to. The longer the book and the longer the opportunity for him to develop any particular personality, be it male or female, the more we believe. And the more we believe the more we come to like or dislike, depending on Fleming's intentions.

He shines as a novelist, or 'book-length' writer, but not with the short story. I think the proof of this is apparent in the sales of his works. With the possible exception of one other title, I would guess that *For Your Eyes Only* has sold far less than the rest. Incredible as it may seem, there *are* people who have never heard of it. It follows, naturally, that they have never heard of Lisl Baum, either. I am sorry to have to say such a thing about a Fleming girl, but I don't think they have missed much.

In the author's next offering to an impatient public he reverted to his true *métier,* the full-length James Bond adventure. Anyone who thought that he might be slipping was obliged to revise his opinion. In *Thunderball* (1961), we have a magnificent work of the imagination. All of the usual ingredients are there: plenty of sex, more than a little sadism, and a modicum of snobbery—if by that particular term the master's detractors mean a considerable dwelling on the activities of monied people in expensive hotels and restaurants, with detailed descriptions of mouth-watering meals.

The book starts with James Bond in a pretty rough physical state. What with his sixty cigarettes a day, too much drinking and a pretty consistent burning of the candle all over, this is not surprising. M has just got his last medical report, and it looks bad. M has just spent a week or two at a private nature-cure establishment down in Sussex, and he's got a bit of a bee in his bonnet about the place. Bond must go there, too, and be 'decarbonized'. James doesn't like this decision, but there is no appeal.

Things look a bit different once he has arrived. For a start, he has hardly been inside the place for more than a few minutes before he almost literally bumps into a pretty girl. Immediately afterwards a car comes swinging round the drive and nearly knocks her down. His reflexes are still fairly good: 'At one moment she was almost under its wheels, at the next, Bond, with one swift step, had gathered her up by the waist and, executing a passable Veronica, with a sharp swivel of the hips had picked her body literally off the bonnet of the car.' So Bond makes a friend right away. He gets a little bonus, too. 'His right hand held the memory of one beautiful breast.'

The girl's name is Patricia Fearing, and she is on the staff down there at 'Shrublands'.

> She was an athletic-looking girl whom Bond would have casually associated with tennis, or skating, or show-jumping. She had the sort of firm, compact figure that always attracted him and a fresh open-air type of prettiness that would have been commonplace but for a wide, rather passionate mouth and a hint of authority that would be a challenge to men.

Patricia is decently clothed at the time—rather unusual for a Bond girl at this stage of his career—and she is dressed in a white smock. But 'it was clear from the undisguised curves of her breasts and hips that she had little on underneath it.' Well, if his winning streak has finished at last we can say he got a place, anyway.

The girl turns out to be some sort of osteopath. After Bond has gone through the rigours of massage and Sitz baths elsewhere, he finds himself delegated to *her* tender mercies. The usual procedure is now reversed. She says: 'Take off your clothes, please. Everything except your pants.' He complies, and then submits to an intensive going-over, but the inversion of the more normal male-female relationship is not lost on him. He 'soon realized that she was an extremely powerful girl. His muscled body, admittedly unresistant, seemed to be easy going for her. Bond felt a kind of resentment at the neutrality of this relationship between an attractive girl and a half naked man.' Any male who has been in a similar situation can appreciate his feelings.

But Bond doesn't submit for long. Being in close proximity to an attractive girl, albeit therapeutically, he can't resist a try. He snatches a kiss and just avoids getting a hard slap across the face. After all, Patricia *is* still on duty.

Bond would not be Bond if he didn't get himself into some sort of trouble or other, even in as quiet and as ostensibly peaceful a place as 'Shrublands'. This time he almost gets himself torn limb from limb on something called a traction table. Recovering, he receives ministrations from Patricia, who, apart from giving him treatment called effleurage, also gives him brandy. Since dandelion tea seems to be the staple drink in this establishment, Bond is impressed.

> Patricia Fearing stood in front of him, clean, white, comfortable, desirable. In one hand was a pair of heavy mink gloves, but with fur covering the palm instead of the back. In the other was a glass. She held out the glass. As Bond drank and heard the reassuring, real-life tinkle of the ice, he thought: this is a most splendid girl. I will settle down with her. She will give me effleurage all day long and from time to time a good tough drink like this. It will be a life of great beauty. He smiled at her and held out the empty glass and said, 'More.'

He doesn't settle down, of course. He hasn't got the time or the opportunity, even if he really had the inclination, which is doubtful. Bond does find time, however, before he leaves 'Shrublands', to score successfully with Patricia, high up on the Sussex downs. Then he is off on the main business of the adventure, and Patricia Fearing is only a memory.

Duty whips Bond from rural England to sophisticated Bermuda: specifically to Nassau and one Domino Vitali. Cars are now playing an increasingly important part in his introductions to pretty girls. I am reminded of Tilly in her little Triumph, and of the indiscreet glimpse of white thigh, Mary Ann Russell in her old Peugeot 403, who starts him dreaming, and Patricia Fearing, nearly knocked down by a reckless Bentley, and Bond's subsequent handful of beautiful breast. Domino drives a sapphire blue two-seater through the streets of Nassau like a Stirling Moss. She is obviously going to be a sympathetic character, because she executes 'an admirable racing change through third into second.' If she were not, I feel sure she would have been like the foxy and pimpled youth who drove Bond to 'Shrublands', and who 'did an expert but unnecessary racing change round an island'.

Be that as it may, Domino is an altogether different proposition from that pimply young taxi-driver back in Sussex. Driving abilities quite aside, she can do things denied to him. 'Not bothering to open the low door of the MG, the girl swung one brown leg and then the other over the side of the car, showing her thighs under the pleated cream cotton skirt almost to her waist, and slipped to the pavement.'

Fortuitously, Bond is an interested onlooker at this delicious moment. (Isn't he always?) His adroitness in the subsequent inevitable pick-up is nothing less than superb. He then

His Women

suggests a drink together, and Domino agrees. They drive off in her car. Since she is at the wheel he has ample opportunity to study her. He knows quite a lot about her already, by the way. That morning he had gone through a hundred immigration forms. It speaks worlds for Bond's memory and concentration that with no previous warning that he was going to run into this girl he can now remember her name, her nationality, her birthplace, her age, her profession—'actress'—and that she is the mistress of a wealthy yacht-owner, Emilio Largo. What he didn't know till now, of course, is that she conforms *à la* Fleming, so to speak. 'She wore no rings and no jewellery except for a rather masculine square gold wrist-watch with a black face. Her flat heeled sandals were of white doeskin. They matched her broad white doeskin belt and the sensible handbag that lay, with a black and white striped silk scarf, on the seat between them.'

Domino is a good driver. She drives like a man. If this appears to be too general a description, let it be understood that Fleming tells us, in a masterly paragraph, how a *woman* drives. Since Bond doesn't have to worry about the usual feminine vacillations at the wheel he is able to inspect her 'without inhibition', and he arrives at some interesting conclusions. He decides that her face 'would become animal in passion. In bed she would fight and bite and then suddenly melt into hot surrender.' All in all, Domino Vitali seems to be quite a girl.

> ...The profile, the straight, uptilted nose, the determined set of the chin, and the clean-cut sweep of the jawline were as decisive as a royal command, and the way the head was set on the neck had the same authority—the poise one associates with imaginary princesses. Two features modified the clean-cut purity of line—a soft, muddled Brigitte Bardot haircut that escaped from under the straw hat in an endearing disarray, and two deeply cut but soft dimples which could only have been etched by a sweet if rather ironic smile that Bond had not yet seen...The general impression...was of a wilful, high-tempered sensual girl—a beautiful Arab marc who would only allow herself to be ridden by a horseman with steel thighs and velvet hands, and then only with curb and saw-bit—and then only when he had broken her to bridle and saddle. Bond thought that he would like to try his strength against hers. But that must be for some other time. For the moment another man was in the saddle. He would first have to be unhorsed.

Domino also has a limp, which Bond finds endearing. One leg is an inch shorter than the other.

If she sounds ultra-sophisticated, another 'luxus whore' just wholeheartedly intent upon a good time, as Bond sees her: 'wilful, high-tempered, sensual', and as we might: without 'such stuff as dreams are made on', don't prejudge her. Later on, drinking with Bond in the Nassau Casino, in a chapter Fleming aptly calls 'Cardboard Hero', she orders a packet of Player's, and for four pages she weaves a fantasy around the bearded salt depicted on the carton. It is a capricious digression on Ian Fleming's part, yes, but it serves its purpose. It does the job. We now see Domino as she *really* is.

Strictly speaking, this girl is on the other side. She is the mistress of Largo, and he's the man Bond is after. Her allegiance is transferred in a unique manner. First of all, Bond makes a rendezvous with her on a deserted beach, for a swim. Domino thinks it is an assignation preliminary to a little cheating, obviously, but to Bond it is business. He feels a twinge or two, being 'excited about the girl, but knowing what he was going to do to her life that afternoon. It was going to be a bad business—when it could have been so good.'

During the swim, Domino gets a couple of sea-egg spines in her foot. Bond picks her up and carries her out of the water. He looks down into her face. 'The bright eyes said yes. He bent his head and kissed her hard on the half-open, waiting mouth.' Then, up to the beach and in the shade of the casuarinas, he proceeds to remove the sea-egg spines.

> The mounded vee of the bikini looked up at Bond and the proud breasts in the tight cup were two more eyes. Bond felt his control going. He said roughly, 'Turn over.'
>
> She did as she was told. Bond knelt down and picked up her right foot... he bent and put his lips to where the black spines showed. He sucked hard for about a minute.

He has to do a bit of biting, too. But he gets the offending spines out with a little trouble. He hurts her, naturally, and he makes her cry. Domino admits that he is the first man who has ever made her do so. This accomplishment, together with what looks suspiciously like a little sadism and masochism, with perhaps a bit of foot-fetishism thrown in, not entirely surprisingly has an aphrodisiacal effect on them both. He picks her up and takes her into the bathing hut. So

His Women

much, then, for all that Bond fantasy hoo-hah about riding her with curbs and saw-bits, and breaking her to bridles and saddles. She didn't need much breaking, and she isn't too difficult to ride.

> ... She kept her arms round his neck while he undid the single button of the brassière and then the tapes of the taut slip. He stepped out of his bathing trunks and kicked them away.

Later, after they have had another swim—this time in the nude—Bond gets down to serious business. He tells Domino that her brother, whom she loved, is dead, and that Largo is responsible for his death. From then on, of course, he has an ally right in the enemy camp, ready to do anything he wants—that is, if she can hold herself back from sticking a shiv into Largo the minute she sees him.

Domino does manage to control herself, but she is strictly an amateur at this cloak and dagger lark, and she gives the game away, notwithstanding. The poor girl gets herself tied to a double bunk on the yacht, 'offered like a starfish, her ankles and wrists strapped to the four corners of the iron work below the mattress.' In almost any other book of this kind, by any author other than Fleming, I think Domino would have been saved in the nick of time. Not here. Largo is after information, and he thinks he knows how to get it. He has a lighted cigar and a bowl of ice-cubes to hand, and very soon a near-naked body to go to work on.

We are not given further details, but who needs them? Suffice it to say that Domino endures much, lives through it all and gains a lovely revenge. In the last chapter of *Thunderball* it is a debatable point whether she or James Bond is in the worse physical shape. 'Someone has ill-treated her,' says a doctor. 'She is suffering from burns—many burns. She is still in great pain.' Bond just about has the strength to rise from his own hospital bed and stagger to hers, in the adjoining room. But neither of them is exactly in the mood nor the condition for carnality just now. He passes out on the rug beside the bed.

> The girl watched the dark, rather cruel face for a moment. Then she gave a small sigh, pulled the pillow to the edge of the bed so that it was just above him, laid her head down so that she could see him whenever she wanted to, and closed her eyes.

I bet M gave Bond 'passionate' leave again after that little lot, but I also bet it was a week or two before either Domino or our James felt like using it.

Of these very unusual books, I think that *The Spy Who Loved Me* (1962) is the most unusual of all. It marked a new departure for Ian Fleming. Hitherto, he has played the part of God, so to speak, looking down upon his remarkable creation and describing Bond's thoughts and actions in the third person. He did it well, better than any of his contemporaries, in my submission. I think there is little doubt that he could have gone on for many years doing much the same sort of thing, and making lots of money each time he published a new title. He must have known that by for once declining to give his public 'the mixture as before' he would receive a great deal of adverse criticism and that his sales would drop.

I admire Ian Fleming for attempting what he did attempt. But when I first read the book I did not. Conditioned to expecting narratives written to something of a formula, as far as the broad plot is concerned, this book had a disturbing effect on me as well as on a great many others. For a start, James Bond does not make an appearance in it until more than halfway through it, and *The Spy Who Loved Me* is by no means another *From Russia, With Love*. Then again, when Bond does show up, we get little of that engaging character-drawing we have come to expect, hokum though it may be. No cocktails, 'shaken, not stirred', no new information about Bond's fads and prejudices, and not a sign of M and the old crowd at Universal Export. This time we get a yarn purportedly written by the girl in the case, and so every observation, every description of her adventures is set down as it is seen by her.

This device even extends to the blurb on the dust-jacket. 'This is the story of who I am and how I came through a nightmare of torture and the threat of rape and death to a dawn of ecstasy. It's all true—absolutely. Otherwise Mr. Fleming certainly would not have risked his professional reputation in acting as my co-author and persuading his publishers, Jonathan Cape, to publish my story.' I'm not so sure about that. True or not, in my opinion Mr. Fleming *did* risk his professional reputation. He could afford to, at this stage of his career, but that's neither here nor there.

Notice the trite jargon in this blurb—written by Fleming himself? Certainly approved by him, anyway. His task, from this dust-jacket onwards, is to maintain subtly the same sort of thing throughout more than two hundred pages. Now this is no easy job. I, perhaps, am being equally trite in my own particular way, but at least it does come naturally. It couldn't have done with *The Spy Who Loved Me*.

It has been suggested that in this book Ian Fleming had dried up, that he had no ideas for a lengthy James Bond adventure in the usual tradition, and that he foisted on to a gullible public a well-padded novelette liberally sprinkled with sexy interludes, finally chucking Bond into the spree as something of a sop. Certainly, the pattern of the book is so different from the others that at first glance it does look as if this criticism might be partly true. But Fleming wasn't the first popular author to deviate from a well-tried formula. Conan Doyle, it should be remembered, tried something of the sort in *The Valley of Fear*. This is one of the four famous Sherlock Holmes 'long' stories, but there isn't a whiff of the famous detective in more than half of the book, but I have never heard of anyone complaining very much on that score. Again, Sapper adopted the first person narrative style in *The Final Count*, the fourth and last of Bulldog Drummond's rounds with Carl Peterson. It wasn't absolutely necessary to the story. I feel that Sapper did it primarily to give us a new slant on his hero: Drummond at work as seen from the point of view of a complete outsider, an ordinary little man drawn by circumstances into a fantastic adventure with this hulking, imperious character.

I believe that Fleming had much the same idea in mind. He had already created a living being with whom we had thrilled and rollicked closely through some eight lengthy escapades. We had watched Bond's exploits, his hazards and his amours with a perennial, all-seeing eye, benign observers aware of his history, of his everyday habits and even of his thoughts. But how would he appear to a frightened and bewildered girl caught up in a nightmarish ordeal with no-one to turn to for help? How would he look through the eyes of this somewhat silly and romantic chit when he suddenly and quite accidentally walked in out of the stormy night to save her?

And Vivienne Michel *is* a silly, romantic chit. Fleming spends the first third of the book developing her, and that fact is fully established as far as I am concerned. My main criticism of *The Spy Who Loved Me* is that too much time is spent on the maudlin reminiscences of her past life before she eventually got into the fix she did, and yet I am obliged to admit that this is the way such a girl *would* relate a narrative. The impact of James Bond on her life at this crucial moment is so great that in the later telling of it all it is necessary for her to inform us in detail of the other men she had known, for comparison's sake.

Vivienne Michel is a French-Canadian Catholic, orphaned in infancy and brought up by a Protestant aunt. Her spiritual conflict that follows may well be imagined, but it is far better described by Fleming. Let no-one sell him short in the matter of succinct elucidation. If anything, he is here too succinct, too lucid, but—lest we forget—this tale is one of 'co-authorship'. It is *by* Ian Fleming, *with* Vivienne Michel. Steam-iron in hand, he smoothes out all the kinks and folds in the newly-washed bed-linen of her memory.

Still—'the fact remains that I arrived in England loaded with a sense of guilt and "indifference" that, added to my "colonialism", were dreadful psychological burdens with which to face a smart finishing school for young ladies.'

Vivienne relates her adolescent life near Sunningdale, the European holidays, the 'coming out', and the usual round of dances and social occasions. Then comes, of course, her first love, and its disillusionment. *I* could see that Derek was a nasty bastard from the very start: why on earth couldn't silly Viv? Are mid-twentieth century virgins of eighteen so dumb? This Derek, at approximately her same age, is known at the '400' nightclub in London and has his own gin bottle there. But he is—presumably—still a schoolboy at Eton, albeit in his last term. Finished with school, he runs a second-hand MG, 'doing quite unnecessary racing changes on the flattest curves'. That makes him a no-goodnik in *my* book right away.

A stone-blind reader with only the vaguest knowledge of braille would know that Derek is after his oats and nothing more, but not Vivienne Michel. She is lured into the box of a back-street Windsor cinema, 'showing two Westerns, a cartoon and so-called "News" that consisted of what the Queen had been doing a month ago.' Why did Viv acquiesce? I know of far more salubrious places not a hundred miles from the Portobello Road and Victoria Station. If I were a girl of eighteen I would hesitate to enter them unaccompanied: with a Derek I should certainly steer clear of a box.

Vivienne's worldly escort turns out to be not so worldly after all. After having gained the girl's somewhat apprehensive consent to let him make love to her, he leaves the box to visit an all-night chemist for a contraceptive. When he comes back he tells her that he didn't know what to ask for! 'I finally said, "One of those things for not having babies. You know."'

I suppose it is inevitable that this pair should be caught *in flagrante delicto* by the manager of the cinema, and chucked out. Vivienne, not surprisingly, is terribly upset and ashamed about it all. You would think she had had enough for one night, but she is so fond of Derek that she allows him to take her into a secluded grove along the river. Here, in sordid surroundings and with considerable misgivings, she is clumsily initiated into the delights of physical love.

> ... I watched the moonlight filtering down through the branches, and tried to stop my tears. So that was it! The great moment. A moment I would never have again. So now I was a woman and the girl was gone! And there had been no pleasure, only pain like they all said. But there remained something. This man in my arms. I held him more tightly to me. I was his now, entirely his, and he was mine. He would look after me. We belonged. Now I would never be alone again. There were two of us.

Not for long, though. This is the last time she ever sees him. He does have the decency to write to her and brush her off completely. He tells her that she is far too good for someone like him. One is inclined to agree. She gets over it, in due course. 'Well, it took just ten minutes to break my heart and about another six months to mend it.'

The next young man to take advantage of her is, if anything, more unpleasant than the first. He is a handsome blond beast named Kurt Rainer, and she works for him. Vivienne becomes his mistress, but theirs is a cold and impersonal affair at best. Kurt is kind and attentive enough in a humourless, Teutonic way—that is, until the girl becomes pregnant. Vivienne doesn't choose the best of times to tell him. He is just about to leave her bedroom. *He* is fully dressed, while *she* is completely naked, and they are just saying a fond goodnight. After the girl has conveyed the tidings, 'he quietly disengaged my arms from round his neck, looked my body up and down with what I can only call a mixture of anger and contempt and reached for the door handle. Then he looked me very coldly in the eyes, said very softly, "So?" and walked out of the room and shut the door quietly behind him.' Nice fellow.

The thing doesn't quite end there. Kurt sends Vivienne to Zürich, where she has an abortion. It's expensive, but Kurt does the big thing. The operation might cost a hundred and fifty pounds, so he gives her a month's salary in lieu of notice. That takes care of a hundred and twenty. Out of the goodness of his heart and out of his own pocket he gives her another fifty. 'Kurt smiled tentatively, waiting for my thanks and congratulations for his efficiency and generosity. He must have been put out by the expression of blank horror on my face...'

Poor, silly little Viv. She does pick the wrong ones. She sums up this unhappy and sordid love affair with a pathetic observation quite in character. 'Before I met Kurt, I had been a bird with a wing down. Now I had been shot in the other.'

Well, the wounded bird does manage to take flight. She sells up her few belongings, buys a Vespa motor-scooter and shoots off to Canada for an extended holiday, leaving all the unhappiness and disillusionment of England behind her. Travelling south from Montreal, she crosses the border into New York State. Here, touring through the Adirondacks, she gets off the beaten track and finally fetches up at a deserted little spot, miles from anywhere, called the Dreamy Pines Motor Court. It is here that the fun really begins.

Circumstances eventually find her all alone and temporarily in charge of the empty motel on a dark and stormy night, with the wind howling through the pines and Vivienne, not unnaturally, a trifle apprehensive. The whole thing is a little bit nightmarish, even before two strange and sinister men turn up out of the wild night. The situation takes on the aspect of a very, very bad dream indeed when it becomes apparent that her two visitors are pyschopathic thugs, obviously with some specific underhand job to do on this very spot. The idea of having a pretty girl with them there, too, is quite pleasant, particularly to one of them. Vivienne is in a perilous position, to put it mildly, with criminal assault just about the best thing she has to look forward to, when who should turn up, of all people?

The whole narrative, to this point, has been a build-up for the entrance of James Bond. If the tale seems an off-beat one for Ian Fleming, I can't agree with those who think this experiment failed. If I were an attractive young girl, confused, unhappy and terrified out of my wits, I think I know how I would feel towards a dark, mysterious and handsome stranger who unexpectedly walked in out of the storm to save me. I would feel much the same as Vivienne, I'm sure.

Bond rescues her from death, and also from that fate worse than death, although they do both get knocked about a bit in the process. What with a fire in the motel and a few cuts and bruises, they feel quite grimy and in need of a bath. Relaxing a little later, they take a shower—together! It's amazing what danger can do to make sexually exciting girls discard their inhibitions and the shackles of convention when Bond is around. A similar sort of thing happened with Gala Brand, you will recall, when the cliff fell on them. Honeychile

Rider, too, cast off all modesty together with her clothes in Dr. No's palatial bathroom. She wanted Bond to wash her, but then his mind was on other things. On this occasion, with Viv, there is no imminent peril: it is Bond who insists on being washed.

> So I bent down and began and of course we were in each other's arms again under the shower and our bodies were slippery with water and soap and he turned the shower off and lifted me out of the shower cabinet and began to dry me lingeringly with the bath towel while I leant back within his free arm and just let it happen.

There now follows a love scene so ardent and shameless that any reader who might earlier have entertained doubts as to whether he was reading a Bond book soon has them quickly dispelled. And Vivienne Michel, only a short while previously trembling at the inevitability of being roughly violated, now has very different views about the matter. 'All women love semi-rape. They love to be taken. It was his sweet brutality against my bruised body that had made his act of love so piercingly wonderful.'

Obviously, it all depends on the man who is raping you.

When we, the readers, first see Tracy—La Comtesse Teresa di Vicenzo—in the very first chapter of *On Her Majesty's Secret Service* (1963), she is dressed in a swim-suit and she is hell-bent on suicide, by drowning. But this is just a sort of flash-back, or should we call it flash-forward? James Bond meets her twenty-four hours *earlier,* but in the second chapter. This time she is fully-clothed, but not surprisingly she is at the wheel of a fast car, a Lancia Flaminia Zagato Spyder, and to judge by the speed at which she's going she is just as intent upon killing herself in a rather different manner.

'If there was one thing that sent James Bond really moving in life, with the exception of gun-play, it was being passed at speed by a pretty girl; and it was his experience that girls who drove competitively were always pretty—and exciting.' Ours too, in his company. So we're off again on another of these fantastic jaunts with Bond, in a book which has already given us a fair proportion of the mandatory requisites in the very first few pages: a beautiful heroine with a kink—this time a death wish—fast cars screaming round S-bends, and a modicum of near-nudity in fashionable surroundings. We are back again at Eaux-les-Royale, for the nonce.

There's a touch of nostalgia here. Bond has forgotten the

adventure of *Casino Royale* no more than we have. 'He had come a long way since then, dodged many bullets and loved many girls, but there had been a drama and a poignancy about that particular adventure that every year drew him back' to this exotic little watering-place on the north coast of France with its casino, its food and the possibility of a romantic meeting with a lovely girl. There's that little churchyard, too, with the grave and the small granite cross that says briefly: 'Vesper Lynd. R.I.P.'

Bond makes Tracy's closer acquaintance, after the car episode, in unique and chivalrous fashion. It's in the casino, and he is in the process of accumulating a packet at *chemin de fer*. She walks in.

'... She had come from nowhere and was standing beside the croupier, and Bond had no time to take in more than golden arms, a beautiful golden face with brilliant blue eyes and shocking pink lips, some kind of plain white dress, a bell of golden hair down to her shoulders, and then it came. 'Banco!'

Yes, she's in on the game as well. The only snag is that when she loses she hasn't got the money to pay up. Consternation! *C'est le coup du dishonneur!* There is a tizzy all round the table. This sort of thing just isn't done. Bond sees the consequences. The girl will be a social outcast for the rest of her life. It's as bad as Sir Hugo Drax cheating at Blade's! He doesn't think any further: he comes to the rescue. 'Bond leant slightly forward. He tossed two of the precious pearly plaques into the centre of the table. He said, with a slightly bored, slightly puzzled intonation, "Forgive me. Madame has forgotten that we agreed to play in partnership this evening ... My mind was elsewhere. Let the game continue."' Good old Bond.

After this, of course, there is no bother at all about joining her and in chatting her up at the table she has chosen to sit at for a drink. He explains to her why he did it, when she asks. Beautiful girl in distress, and all that jazz. In addition, he reminds her that she had passed him on the road in her Lancia only a few hours before and that they had had a little race. He had been thinking of other things at the time, otherwise she would never have passed him. But Tracy doesn't agree. She could always beat him. *He* wants to stay alive.

'Oh, lord! thought Bond. One of those! A girl with a wing, perhaps two wings, down.' Here, here, what's this? Does James Bond read Fleming, too? Vivienne Michel described herself in much the same way only about twelve months earlier!

Tracy isn't interested in conversation. But she is obviously grateful for what he has done, and she knows what he's after, too. As she tells him, he has earned his reward.

> She rose abruptly. So did Bond, confused. 'No. I will go alone. You can come later. The number is 45. There, if you wish, you can make the most expensive piece of love of your life. It will have cost you four million francs. I hope it will be worth it.'

Now James Bond is never one to pass up an opportunity like this, particularly since that four million had been 'found money', anyway. And he's not exactly on duty at the moment and this sort of thing was what he'd been hoping for when he came to Eaux-les-Royale, apart from gambling heavily and guzzling lightly. He accepts the invitation, although not without a qualm or two, for 'this one was in the grip of stresses he could not even guess at.' Shades of Tiffany Case! Screwballs of this nature seem to have a strange effect on Bond. More or less normal beauties are there for the loving and the leaving: the queerer they come the more involved he gets. *Vide* Tracy:

> ... Take off those clothes. Make love to me. You are handsome and strong. I want to remember what it can be like. Do anything you like. And tell me what you like and what you would like from me. Be rough with me. Treat me like the lowest whore in creation. Forget everything else. No questions. Take me.

She's obviously not right. It isn't surprising, I think, that James Bond, the next day, decides to keep an eye on her. Not that he *need* have done, necessarily. Others were on the lookout, too. Her father is a very important man: Marc-Ange Draco, an engaging and benevolent scoundrel who is head of the Union Corse. He has spies and employees everywhere. He knows all about Bond's generous gesture back in the casino, and even about the later events in Tracy's room. But he is not annoyed about it, or even offended. 'A man is a man and, who knows?— ... What you did, the way you behaved in general, may have the beginnings of some kind of therapy.' Well, I suppose that's one way of looking at it.

Draco is really concerned about his daughter. The girl has been through a rough time. Her well-being means a great deal to him. So much so, in fact, that he makes an offer. He wants Bond to court Tracy and marry her. And on the wedding day he will give Bond a personal present of a million pounds in gold!

But nothing doing. For one thing, Bond is quite happy as he is. For another, he doesn't particularly want a million. But he does agree to do whatever he can to help Tracy, not only for her own sake, but for that of her father. Bond and Draco have taken quite a fancy to each other. But marriage is out. What Tracy needs is a spell in a good clinic, probably in Switzerland, to forget her past unhappiness and to regain the will to live. Does Marc-Ange understand?

Draco gets the message. He decides to do as Bond suggests. Meanwhile, is there something he might do for Bond? Draco has 'great resources, great knowledge, great power. They are all yours.' After all, the Union Corse is as influential as the Unione Siciliano or the dreaded Mafia. Now it must never be forgotten that James Bond is first and foremost a Secret Service agent, and that ever since the Thunderball business of a year or two previously he had been continually chasing abortive leads to the sinister head of SPECTRE, who had organized the whole operation, and who had escaped.

> Bond had a flash of inspiration. He smiled broadly. 'There is a piece of information I want. There is a man called Blofeld. Ernst Stavro Blofeld. You will have heard of him. I wish to know if he is alive and where he is to be found.'

Draco knows, roughly. He can tell Bond enough to set the ball rolling, and so we are soon off on the main business of this book, which is that of laying Blofeld by the heels. Tracy is temporarily forgotten. But in the ensuing adventure, much of which takes place high in the Swiss Alps, Bond encounters other gorgeous girls. Ten of them, to be precise. Not that he goes to bed with the lot: that would be *too* much, even for Bond, and even if duty demanded it. But one of them, named Ruby, is an unwitting and convenient aid in a game he is playing to unmask the elusive Blofeld, now calling himself Monsieur le Comte de Bleuville in a scientific research institute on top of a private Alp. In order to winkle certain information out of Ruby, Bond is obliged to pretend that he loves her, although there is no doubt at all that he genuinely has a lech for her. This leads to a clandestine visit to her bedroom. His perquisites are pleasant, and no more than he deserves during the course of a highly-dangerous operation like this one.

> ... A small night wind rose up and moaned round the building, giving an extra sweetness, an extra warmth, even a certain friendship to what was no more than an act of physical passion. There was real pleasure in what they did to each other, and in the end, when it was over and they lay quietly in each other's arms, Bond knew, and knew that the girl knew, that they had done nothing wrong, done no harm to each other.

Bond is extremely fortunate to get off that Alp in one piece. Even so, he could never have got very far on his own, what with the condition he was in, and with Blofeld's men breathing down his neck. What a stroke of luck it is to find among all the Alps in Switzerland, at the foot of this one, as beautiful and as bewitching as ever, one of those people who turn up unexpectedly just when they are needed most. Tracy!

What is it—gratitude, relief, kinship with kinkiness, real love at last? What *is* it that causes Bond to think the matter over very, very carefully and then decide to propose to Tracy? It isn't the possibility of that million pounds from Draco. Of that I'm sure. It couldn't just be sex, either. Bond never needed marriage and a settled existence for an unlimited supply of that particular boon. He does reflect that he is 'fed up with all these untidy, casual affairs' that leave him with a bad conscience, but is he being honest with himself? What about Ruby, such a short while before? He had then been musing upon the fact that they had done no wrong and had done no harm to each other! No pangs of conscience there. Why should they suddenly worry him now?

It's all very well for Bond to go waffling on in his mind about the pleasant prospect of children, and extolling Tracy's virtues to himself. Perhaps she *would* let him get on with his life. Perhaps she *does* love him. All right, maybe she needs him, too, and she *will* be someone for him to look after. But will it ever work? What about those times when M shoots him off on some assignment and the inevitable lovely girl is waiting? Will cheating, in the line of duty, be smiled upon by Tracy Bond? Or does he intend to hand in his double O, to henceforth eschew the atmosphere of adventure and do a routine office job for the Service for the rest of his working life? If so, what about all those married women in London? How about Miss Moneypenny, lying in wait for him at Universal Export these many years? This is just the sort of set-up she's been wanting! And Mary Goodnight, so fresh, so new, so little known as yet to us *or* Bond? Will he be able to resist a try?

Well, it happens. Yes, James Bond marries. There is all the business of rings, of whether they will have twin beds or a double, and of wondering whether he's got enough sheets and pillows back at the flat for two. Imagine Bond going through all that rigmarole! Even so, 'he was surprised to find that all this nest-building gave him a curious pleasure, a feeling that he had at last come to rest and that life would now be fuller, have more meaning, for having someone to share it with. Togetherness! What a curiously valid cliché it was!'

So Fleming fools us after all. He marries Bond off. Why? Well, I wonder. Could it date back to that radio conversation between Fleming and Raymond Chandler, when the American confessed that *he* was marrying off Philip Marlowe? Did it start Fleming thinking? It's just possible.

'I do.'

James Bond said the words at ten-thirty in the morning of a crystal-clear New Year's Day in the British Consul General's drawing-room.

And he meant them.

By a little after twelve he is a widower, and Tracy is a crumpled mass over the steering-wheel of their car, with blood already oozing from the wounds made from Blofeld's bullets.

It's a cruel thing to have to say, but I knew this marriage could never last.

His Adversaries

NO SECRET SERVICE agent, private detective, Scotland Yard policeman or amateur freelance, whether he lived in fact or in fiction, ever came up against as impressive an array of rogues and villains as James Bond. He's had them all: master spies, arch-criminals, paranoiacs and plain, if unordinary gangsters. If it weren't for the fact that he is such a terror with the women there would have been one or two *femmes fatale*, too. But any girl who might be opposing him at the start

His Adversaries

very soon comes over on to his side. I'm not counting Rosa Klebb and Irma Bunt. They were crows, anyway.

As if this Rogues' Gallery were not enough to contend with, Bond has also crossed swords with two powerful organizations: SMERSH, a secret department of the Soviet Government more fully known as Smiert Spionam—Death to Spies—and SPECTRE, which is a sinister contraction of The Special Executive for Counterintelligence, Terrorism, Revenge and Extortion.

Yes, he's had the lot, and so far he's always emerged top dog. It's been touch and go many times with him, and once or twice Bond has been practically scared to death. Yet I think he would almost be prepared to face any one of those villains again rather than be confronted, still with the remains of a hangover, by M on a murky Monday morning.

M is James Bond's foremost adversary. There is a sort of love-hate relationship there. M is his boss, the man who sends him off on all these fantastic exploits, with only the briefest of briefings. Bond continually rebels against his authority—even if it's only in letters of resignation drafted in his mind as he speeds along in his car—but he does rebel. Face to face with the martinet, it's 'Yes, sir,' and 'No, sir.' M can really put the fear of Christ up Bond.

We have never been told M's full name. We don't even know for sure what the letter M actually stands for. Is it just an initial, or something departmental? We know all about the OO section, and we've met the Head of S. There are places like Station C, too. But what about M? It may be just coincidence, of course, but it *is* a fact that both his christian-name and surnames begin with that letter. I am not betraying any confidences when I say that his first name is Miles, and (pause for genuflexion)—he's a 'Sir'. The evidence can be found in the Bond saga, if one is sufficiently interested to look for it.

Although Bond clashes with him often enough, M is no villain. Quite the reverse, in fact. He is rather heroic in his own particular way, which is the way of the Old School. There aren't many of that old school left these days.

M is the head of the British Secret Service, and he runs that amazing organization from behind a desk at the top of a large building near Regent's Park. To the world he appears to be the boss of a queer sort of firm called Universal Export. There's an employee there whose full-time job it is to fob off any stray callers who might want to do some universal exporting. To his juniors M is the perennial skipper, a sort of Old Man. By any standards, he *is* an old man, but there is nothing senile about him yet. At times, he is a lot fitter than

Bond himself. He has 'frosty, damnably clear grey eyes.' He also smokes a pipe—none of these eternal debilitating cigarettes.

Devotion to duty can be the only possible reason why M took on this exacting and highly-responsible job. Like Bond, he is a naval man. In fact, he threw up 'the certain prospect of becoming Fifth Sea Lord in order to take over the Secret Service.' He earns £5,000 a year, 'with the use of an ancient Rolls Royce and the driver thrown in.' He is a retired Vice-Admiral and his pension is probably £1,500. He lives in London, but he also rents a small Regency house on Crown Lands near Windsor Forest. M calls this place Quarterdeck. Naturally, he would *prefer* to live by the sea.

He is unmarried and, except for servants, he lives alone. For all we are told to the contrary, he has done so ever since he left the navy. He appears to be morally scrupulous to an extraordinarily high degree, particularly where sex is concerned. Although he must be a bit past that sort of thing now, anyway, M is a character sufficiently real to lead one to speculate a little about his private life. On the face of things, he *seems* almost as emasculated as the Terrible Trio, with whom he has so much else in common, but remember that M is a creature of Ian Fleming's. And, after all, you know what sailors are . . .

My opinion is the either M is undersexed or that he sublimates like mad. And if I appear to be somewhat preoccupied with the hormonic factor in these Fleming characters, let it be understood that others far more illustrious and responsible than I have dwelt on this matter, too. Some have speculated orally and imaginatively, if privately, like gossiping girlies at a hen-party. I've seen it. Others proclaim their opinions abroad. Cyril Connolly, for instance, has allowed his fancy certain vagaries about M in public print. Recommended reading—nay, *required* reading—on this matter is his brilliant pastiche, 'Bond Strikes Camp.'* Do I labour the point when I say that in this parody's title the sophisticated reader sees all?

. . . M had certain bees in his bonnet. They were famous in the Service, and M knew they were. But that did not

---

* *Previous Convictions* (Hamish Hamilton, 1963). The first review I read of these essays censured 'Bond Strikes Camp', and deplored Connolly's misuse of his talents. I felt a toe-rag for liking it. But the second review I saw was wholly written *around* this piece, and was eulogistic. This doesn't vindicate me, but it is comforting to know that there is another toe-rag in the book world.

His Adversaries

mean that he would allow them to stop buzzing. There were queen bees, like the misuse of the Service, and the search for true as distinct from wishful intelligence, and there were worker bees. These included such idiosyncrasies as not employing men with beards, or those who were completely bilingual, instantly dismissing men who tried to bring pressure to bear on him through family relationships with members of the Cabinet, mistrusting men or women who were too 'dressy', and those who called him 'sir' off-duty; and having an exaggerated faith in Scotsmen.

Well, I fancy M must mistrust Bond quite a bit, on the quiet. For one thing, Bond is more than a little particular about the clothes he puts on—I'd call him dressy, although Fleming might not. For another thing, I just can't imagine him dreaming of calling M anything but 'sir', whatever the circumstances. Admittedly, Bond *did* relax a little on one of the very few occasions that we are privileged to find them together on off-duty hours: that famous dinner at Blade's. Possibly Bond was making an effort to be particularly informal? M 'Jamesed' him quite a bit: Bond teetered on the tight-rope—not too frosty, not too free. Yet a 'sir' did creep in, even then. Still, whether or not M *does* mistrust Bond, he *has* got a lot of faith in the man: Bond is half Scottish.*

Whenever he is called into that inner sanctum of M's, Bond can usually tell whether it's for a job or not. If the interview is official, M normally calls him '007'; if it's not, he is 'James'. M rarely varies from this approach. Once, when the old man roped Bond in and enlisted his services for a private, extracurricular job, he gave the game away right from the start by using the christian name. As Bond reflects, M recruiting anyone 'on a personal matter must have seemed to him like stealing the Government's money.'

A few hours later when this private job has unexpectedly turned official, Bond is straight away '007' again, with no nonsense.

On another occasion, when M is asking after Bond's current heart-throb, and hears that the romance is off, he says: 'I'm sorry if it went wrong, James.' But there is no sympathy in his voice. He had only asked that question to see if Bond was fancy-free to tackle a ticklish proposition concerning another young lady. The moment M knows Bond *is* free, our man is a number again.

* Or wholly? At the time of writing, this had yet to be determined.

To digress for just a moment on the subject of nomenclature, why is it that Bond must always be *James* when not on duty? M, who knows him better than many, has never attempted a familiar diminutive even in his more warm and expansive moments. To May, Bond's housekeeper, as one who always knows her place, her employer would never be less than Mr. James. Bond cohabits with countesses and chorus girls, but not one of them has yet called him Jim, Jimmy or Jimmikins. I fear for the one who first does. Be it amid the beguilements of the boudoir or on a Pullman in the full flood of priapic passion a quick slosh across the chops will be her portion, I fancy.

But to return to M. Although he is Bond's senior, I suppose he is the nearest thing to a sort of Dr. Watson that these books will ever have.* And that's not very near, admittedly. But I think he is the one main character who puts in an appearance in nearly all of them. He is as real and as alive as Bond himself, even if he is *just* a little larger than life itself. In the films he is portrayed by the actor Bernard Lee, and in my opinion this piece of casting is the only bad piece. Lee does the job capably enough, of course, but he just isn't M. He is far too young, for one thing. For another, he doesn't look the part. Not to me, anyway. Sean Connery is James Bond, all right, and I think perhaps he always was, in my mind's eye. But I shall always visualize M as I first imagined him: something like that hoary old martinet of an English gentleman created and played by C. Aubrey Smith in so many Hollywood films before and during the war.

Proceeding to Bond's adversaries proper, the villains he encounters either by accident or design, Le Chiffre is the first whose malfeasances, malpractices and dirty-doggeries are fully documented. Strictly speaking, though, he wasn't really a villain at all at the start of *Casino Royale*. He was an unpleasant bit of work, yes, but he had done no harm to Bond, to M, or to the Head of S, who cooked up the plan to destroy him. It was purely a matter of self defence that turned Le Chiffre so nasty.

He was a Soviet agent and the paymaster of a French, communist-controlled trade union. He was unwise enough to borrow from the union funds some fifty million francs to purchase control of a chain of brothels. This wasn't exactly ethical, of course, but it still can't be called very villainous by Secret Service standards. Anyway, 'it is possible that Le Chiffre was motivated more by a desire to increase his union

---

* 'Obit:' informs us that there has been another all along. But he kept himself well in the background.

His Adversaries

funds than by the hope of lining his own pocket by speculating with his employers' money. However that may be, it is clear that he could have found many investments more savoury than prostitution, if he had not been tempted by the by-product of unlimited women for his personal use.'

Le Chiffre had hardly taken over this potentially profitable little business before a French law was passed closing down all the brothels in the country. No doubt he could have salvaged something, in the ordinary way of things, but the Deuxième Bureau soon got wind of the 'significance of the situation', and they started hounding him right and left. In a few months he had nothing—nothing but a deficit of fifty million francs and the imminent possibility of a routine inquiry from Leningrad regarding his union's finances.

'... Le Chiffre plans, we believe, to follow the example of most other desperate till-robbers and make good the deficit in his accounts by gambling,' says the memorandum passed from the Head of S to M. The Secret Service has accumulated all this information about his activities and intentions from an agent of theirs in France: a Eurasian mistress of Le Chiffre.'* With the remaining capital of the union, twenty-five million francs, he intends to try and make another fifty million by baccarat at Eaux-Les-Royale and so save his skin.

The plan devised by the Head of S is to send a good man over, bolstered by sufficient funds, to out-gamble him. The idea behind it is to discredit Le Chiffre, to ridicule him and to destroy him and, incidentally, to bankrupt his trade union. Simple assassination would be pointless: Le Chiffre would become a martyr. The whole thing is a gamble in itself—even at the very best. But it's worth a try. The man sent out to do the job is James Bond.

They really fight their battles with the gloves off in the Secret Service. There are no gentlemanly agreements about not hitting a man when he is down, and all that sort of rot. This is a cold-blooded plot to destroy a man, just as is the *konspiratsia* against Bond himself, some years later, in *From Russia, With Love*. The one big difference is that the opposition is very, very acute, and they know all about Bond right from the very start, and probably even before he arrives in Eaux-les-Royale. All's fair in love and war, so Le Chiffre has a shot at eliminating Bond by means of a little bomb-throwing. This doesn't come off, but it shows our side just how desperate Le Chiffre really is. As James Bond says, 'The

---

* Females always seem to get the dirty end of the stick. Bond has had his unpleasant moments, but duty has never demanded, yet, that he bed down with a partner so physically unattractive as Le Chiffre.

opposition has got me... all weighed up and it seems no holds are going to be barred.'

If it were not for Ian Fleming's descriptions of meals, of love scenes, of car chases and of fights, I should be almost inclined to say that he is at his most absorbing when he is writing about a game at the card table for very high stakes. The baccarat battle of Bond versus Le Chiffre is the very first example of this particular virtuosity we get, and it is one of the best. In fact, not a *great* deal of excitement happens in this book away from the card table. I should think that *Casino Royale* caught on and paved the way for further Bond adventures as much on two or three fascinating chapters in the middle as on anything else, sex and sadism included.

The upshot is that Le Chiffre gets cleaned out. Up to this point he hasn't exactly been chivalrous, but it is only now that he *really* begins to turn nasty. He captures Bond and his assistant—the delectable Vesper Lynd—and takes them both to his villa. In order to squeeze an answer out of Bond regarding the whereabouts of the money he needs so desperately, he puts into practice a torture device of such mundane originality that many a Fleming devotee recalls it when others in the later books have been forgotten.

The instruments of persuasion are an armchair with its seat removed and a three-foot-long carpet-beater in twisted cane. Bond is completely unclothed. He is made to sit in the chair and is tightly bound to it with flex.

> ...the knots...left no play in any of the bindings. All of them bit sharply into Bond's flesh. The legs of the chair were broadly spaced and Bond could not even rock it.
>
> He was utterly a prisoner, naked and defenceless.
>
> His buttocks and the under part of his body protruded through the seat of the chair towards the floor.
>
> ...Le Chiffre lit a cigarette and swallowed a mouthful of coffee from the glass. Then he picked up the cane carpet-beater and, resting the handle comfortably on his knee, allowed the flat trefoil base to lie on the floor directly under Bond's chair.
>
> He looked Bond carefully, almost caressingly, in the eyes. Then his wrist sprang suddenly upwards on his knee.
>
> The result was startling.

I imagine so. Particularly for James Bond. Le Chiffre points out to him, after he has recovered a little from that

His Adversaries 93

initial flick, that refinements in torture are quite unnecessary. Simple instruments are just as effective as anything elaborate. 'It is not only the immediate agony, but also the thought that your manhood is being gradually destroyed and that at the end, if you will not yield, you will no longer be a man.'

Bond sticks it for about an hour. I don't know how much longer he could have held out, particularly since at this moment Le Chiffre decides to do a little surgery with a carving-knife. The exact nature of this we are not told, but I assume that the projected operation may be euphemistically called by a word I have perhaps overworked somewhat in the foregoing pages: Bond is to be emasculated.

It is a topsy-turvy stroke of irony that Bond should be saved in the nick of time, on this occasion, by one of the greatest of all his adversaries to come, SMERSH itself, no less. This powerful organization has sent out a man to deal with Le Chiffre. 'I have been sent by the Soviet Union to eliminate you ... We cannot see the end of the trouble you have caused.'

The SMERSH agent could have rubbed Bond out, too, as easily as winking. But he doesn't. He has had no orders to do so. But he leaves a trade-mark: he carves a Russian letter on the back of the Secret Service agent's hand, branding him as a spy to all SMERSH men he might meet in the future. But after what he'd been through, this indignity must have felt like a pin prick. Bond lives to fight another day. For this relief much thanks.

James Bond is a glutton for punishment. That ordeal on the French coast would have cured most men of a taste for dangerous living. Not Bond.

It is said that one has no actual *memory* of pain. I suppose this must be true. How else to explain a woman's second, third and fourth essay into childbirth? How else to explain a not particularly successful boxer's continued dedication to his chosen profession, or, rather more simply, our regular visits to the dentist, which are rarely wholly painless? Indeed, how else to explain James Bond's perverse adherence to a career so agonizing?

Early on in *Live and Let Die* we find him savouring sweet revenge on SMERSH for that cut on the hand. Dastardly ingrate. He wouldn't be here now if that agent hadn't stepped in and saved his life. After all, plastic surgery had now fixed up the scars on his hand, 'painlessly but slowly.' It must be the indignity of the thing that rankles. He is driving to a summons from M:

... and as Bond thought of the man with the stiletto who had cut them he clenched his hands on the wheel.

What was happening to the brilliant organization of which the man with the knife had been an agent... Was it still as powerful, still as efficient?... Bond had sworn to get back at them. He had told M as much at that last interview. Was this appointment with M to start him on his trail of revenge?

Well, what do you think? Of course it is. Lots of gold coins, all minted before 1650, have been turning up recently in the United States. They look like part of the treasure-trove accumulated by the old pirates, Bloody Morgan in particular. One of them is a Rose Noble* of Edward IV.

All this stuff is coming into the States, and Station C is extraordinarily interested in a certain yacht which is operating from Jamaica way through the Florida Keys to St. Petersburg, on the west coast of Florida. It seems that the owner of this yacht is a certain Mr. Big. Says M: '"... a negro gangster. Lives in Harlem. Ever heard of him?" "No," says Bond.'

If you're with me so far, *you* have. It appears that this treasure is being used to finance Soviet espionage, or some of it, anyway, in America.

'Mr. Big,' said M, weighing his words, 'is probably the most powerful negro criminal in the world. He is,' and he enumerated carefully, 'the head of the Black Widow Voodoo cult and believed by that cult to be the Baron Samedi himself. (You'll find all that here,' he tapped the folder, 'and it'll frighten the daylights out of you.) He is also a Soviet agent. And finally he is, and this will particularly interest you, Bond, a known member of SMERSH.'

'Yes,' said Bond slowly, 'I see now.'

So do we. Ian Fleming has us in his merciless grip.

Mr. Big's real name is Buonaparte Ignace Gallia. Those initials did a lot to give him his now more familiar name, but his size helped just as much. He stands six feet six and weighs twenty stone. Born in Haiti, half negro and half French, he is no ordinary criminal. Mr. Big is highly intelli-

---

* If only to show off my ignorance, I should like to remind readers of Dornford Yates that his most villainous scoundrel was called 'Rose' Noble. Until I read *Live and Let Die* I always wondered why.

His Adversaries

gent, was initiated into Voodoo as a child and has since put this sinister cult to excellent use. Starting an underground Voodoo temple in Harlem, he did his best to encourage the idea that he is the Zombie of the dreaded Baron Samedi, the Prince of Darkness. On the strength of this alone he holds thousands of employees and agents in a grip of fear, as well as a great many other superstitious and semi-literate coloured folk.

He built up quite a criminal organization in New York before the war, graduating somewhat in the style of Al Capone and eliminating opposition or obstacles ruthlessly to consolidate his position. I can understand his being called up for military service in 1943, but I fail to understand why he didn't dodge the draft. It would have been simple for a man like this. But, accepting that he did don a uniform for the duration, I find it hard to accept that even so fine a linguist as he could have been trained and employed by the o.s.s., what with his record of bootlegging and the vice racket. And yet, I suppose even beggars like the Secret Service authorities can't be choosers in wartime. He disappeared for five years after the war, and it is assumed that he must have gone to Moscow. But he returned to Harlem in 1950 with a seemingly inexhaustible supply of funds and very quickly established himself again with a chain of brothels. But now he had the FBI on his tail: he was a suspected Soviet agent.

When James Bond encounters him, Mr. Big is sitting pretty. Washington knows all about him, but they haven't got a thing on him. They can't touch him. His negro hordes fear him, but not one of them tries to kill him. How can you? He's a Zombie: he's already dead.

Bond's first close look at this fearsome creature is under poor conditions. He is Mr. Big's prisoner.

> It was a great football of a head, twice the normal size and very nearly round. The skin was grey-black, taut and shining like the face of a week-old corpse in the river. It was hairless, except for some grey-brown fluff above the ears. There were no eyebrows and no eyelashes and the eyes were extraordinarily far apart so that one could not focus on them both, but only one at a time. Their gaze was very steady and penetrating. When they rested on something they seemed to devour it, to encompass the whole of it. They bulged slightly and the irises were golden round black pupils which were now wide. They were animal eyes, not human, and they seemed to blaze.

Beside this monster, Le Chiffre appears to me as mild and harmless as a Sunday school teacher.

In fact, in my opinion, *Live and Let Die* is an altogether different proposition from *Casino Royale* in many respects. That first book was good, but now, on re-reading all of them, it is apparent that Ian Fleming was merely serving an apprenticeship with that initial essay into sensational fiction. This second book is far superior in characterization, in pace and in excitement. Some of its descriptions I find enthralling. While I have never thought that Fleming was at his best when writing about America and Americans, I believe that his Harlem chapters in this book are some of his finest. 'Nigger Heaven' and 'Table Z', while not entirely necessary to the narrative, are absolutely essential to the atmosphere, and his handling of urban negro dialect is, to me, completely convincing.

Its printing history alone is sufficient gauge of this book's success, yet although it has the seductive Solitaire and there are moments of cerebral titillation for the reader where she is concerned, it has never sold on its erotic content. There is not a copulation in it from start to finish. In 1961, when *Thunderball* was published, Jonathan Cape saw fit to append opposite the title page not only the eight previous James Bond adventures, but details of their impressions. *Live and Let Die* had been reprinted seven times in hard covers alone: considerably more than any of the other titles. Things have probably changed a little now. The film versions of two of the books have seen to that.

I suppose that if there is any truth at all in the charge that these books are a compound of sex, sadism and snobbery, the sadistic element overwhelmingly predominates here.

'Which finger do you use least, Mister Bond?'

Bond was startled by the question. His mind raced.

'On reflection, I expect you will say the little finger of the left hand,' continued the soft voice. 'Tee-Hee, break the little finger of Mr. Bond's left hand.'

The negro showed the reason for his nickname.

'Hee-hee,' he gave a falsetto giggle. 'Hee-hee.'

He walked jauntily over to Bond...

The finger stood upright, away from the hand. Started to bend slowly backwards towards his wrist. Suddenly it gave. There was a sharp crack.

'That will do,' said Mr. Big.

Tee-Hee released the mangled finger with reluctance.

Bond uttered a soft animal groan and fainted.

His Adversaries

'Da guy ain't got no sensayuma,' commented Tee-Hee.

This is an example. Mr. Big also gives instructions for Bond's accomplice, Felix Leiter, to be damaged somewhat similarly. But if Fleming were content merely to offer us sadism and nothing else, he could have easily made Leiter's ordeal as unpleasant as Bond's. At that, he *does* give us an indication of what *could* have happened to Felix, during a later telephone conversation. 'Blackjack. Knocked out. Nothing serious. They started out by considering all sorts of ingenious things. Wanted to couple me to the compressed air pump in the garage. Start on the ears and then proceed elsewhere.' But Leiter gets to discussing hot music with his captors. The magic names of Duke Ellington and Jelly Roll Morton are invoked. A sort of *cameraderie* is formed. Another triumph for the universality of jazz! In the end all Leiter gets is the blackjack. The negro 'was very apologtic, said it was the least he could have done. I believe him.'

But never forget that this is a Fleming book. Sympathetic characters don't always get away with minor harms and hurts. Heroines die, sometimes. Heroic allies, also. And it is in this book that Felix Leiter, earlier saved from the compressed air pump by a quick wit and a knowledge of jazz records, falls through a trap-door into a tank containing a man-eating shark. 'My books are just out of step,' says Fleming.

Felix lives on today. New readers meeting him for the first time in more recent books might well wonder at the steel hook he uses instead of a hand, at the limp, at the skin grafting, and at the right arm gone and the left leg too, until they read *Live and Let Die*. Hot discography had availed him nothing with that Hammerhead—or was it a Tiger Shark? We have never been told, exactly. Not that it matters particularly. But one recalls the grim joke of Mr. Big's sadistic employee, that pencilled scrawl stuck in the mouth of the mummy-like heap of blood-soaked, dirty bandages containing what was left of Leiter: HE DISAGREED WITH SOMETHING THAT ATE HIM.

'Let the punishment fit the crime,' sang Gilbert's Mikado. Well, Ian Fleming may deal roughly with those of his characters who are on the side of law and order, but he is also drastic with his wrong-doers. They seldom die by the swift and merciful bullet. I should hate to die like Buonaparte Ignace Gallia.

I'm sure it can't be coincidence, but it is a fact that nearly all of James Bond's adversaries are extremely wealthy. Those who are not rich in their own right usually have the backing of organizations like SMERSH, and are bolstered by Moscow Gold. Sir Hugo Drax, the villain of *Moonraker*, is a good example of this tradition. He is a multi-millionaire.

This book is the only one of Bond's adventures with its action taking place wholly in England. Normally, M shoots him off abroad somewhere. Deceptively, one gets the impression that no matter where he may begin, sooner or later he will fetch up somewhere in the Caribbean, much in the same way that Dornford Yates' characters always ended up in Austria or within spitting distance of Pau, in the Pyrenees. Actually, from a total of eleven books—at the time of writing—Bond can be found under a tropical sun in only four. But this is by the way. The nearest we get to places like Kingston or Nassau in *Moonraker* is in a few lines from that old sorehead M, who is glad enough to see Bond back from that convalescence after the Mr. Big imbroglio, but who resents the sun-tan still evident. 'Hope the colour won't last too long. Always suspicious of sunburned men in England. Either they've not got a job of work to do or they put it on with a sun-lamp.' This is all mere chit-chat, really. If M had called Bond in for something big he would have come to the point pretty quickly. As it is he grunts and snaps for a bit and obviously has some difficulty in coming to the point at all. He's embarrassed. Finally he asks if Bond has heard of a chap called Sir Hugo Drax. This is a rather surprising question: everyone knows of the man. It's rather like asking someone in 1964 if they have ever heard of James Bond. M asks for details. 'Just give me the facts as you see them. I'd like to know if your version tallies with mine.' This is an excellent device of Fleming's to draw a thumbnail sketch of Drax for our benefit.

> 'Well, sir,' said Bond finally. 'For one thing the man's a national hero. The public have taken to him. I suppose he's in much the same class as Jack Hobbs or Gordon Richards. They've got a real feeling for him. They consider he's one of them, but a glorified version. A sort of superman. He's not much to look at, with all those scars from his war injuries, and he's a bit loud-mouthed and ostentatious. But they rather like that. Makes him a sort of Lonsdale figure, but more in their class. They like his friends calling him "Hugger" Drax. It makes him a bit of a card and I expect it gives the women a thrill. And then when you think what he's doing for the country, out of his own pocket and far beyond what any government seems to be able to do,

His Adversaries

it's really extraordinary that they don't insist on making him Prime Minister.'

What he is doing for the country is personally financing a super atomic rocket called 'The Moonraker'. He has built up his enormous fortune by cornering 'a very valuable ore called Columbite.' This stuff has a very high melting point, it is essential to the making of jet engines and there isn't much of it in the world. Anyone who wants Columbite has to come to him for it—at his price. He is a national hero because, in a letter to the Queen, he gives his entire holding of the ore to the country, plus £10,000,000, announces that he already has the design of this rocket and is prepared to find the staff to build it.

All in all, Drax appears to be quite a benefactor. ' "Peace in Our Time—This Time." I remember the headline.' M muses a little. ' "... A wonderful story. Extraodinary man." He paused, reflecting. "There's only one thing..." '

Drax, it seems, cheats at cards.

Now M is a member of Blade's, the gambling club, and the chairman has called upon him for help. Nobody else has begun to suspect Drax yet, but he's winning too regularly and far too often, and they play for pretty high stakes at Blade's. A scandal will really put the cat among the pigeons if anybody does suspect. '... And don't forget that cheating at cards can still smash a man. In so-called "Society", it's about the only crime that can still finish you, whoever you are. Drax does it so well that nobody's caught him yet.' The possible repercussions, if someone does, are enormous. The bloody fool's walking a tightrope. The chairman at Blade's foresees all sorts of things: an incident, scandal, resignation, then M.P. members talking about it in the Lobby, a libel action ... The main concern, of course, is that if it *does* come out the whole 'Moonraker' project will be up the spout. Something's got to be done. This is where James Bond comes in. All M wants his man to do is rap the millionaire over the knuckles fairly lightly, give him a taste of his own medicine and make it quietly obvious that he's been tumbled.

Bond, as we know, is something of a whizz at gambling. He'll cheat right and left when it comes to love and women, and he's not adverse to kicking a man when he's down, but he's as straight as a die at cards. There are some things even *he* won't do. But he knows all the tricks. He has learned all the secrets of the card-sharps and he could take any one of them on at his own game and stand a fifty-fifty chance of winning. M knows this: that's why he was so diffident about the whole thing at the start. Bond agrees to observe Drax at play and then meet him on his own terms and teach him a lesson.

Sir Hugo Drax is a lovely creation. He is a loud-mouthed braggart and a bully, the sort of chap not very far removed from that original who inspired the 'even his best friends don't like him' wisecrack. How he ever got into Blade's in the first place is a mystery. It's a very exclusive place: the mere possession of much money doesn't cut a lot of ice there, although you've obviously got to be well-breeched, once you're in, to stand the pace. It must have been because Drax had captured the imagination of the public with his rocket idea and was viewed everywhere as a hero. You have to get to know him personally to see what an utter cad he is.

Ian Fleming has treated us to some queer-looking characters in his time. Le Chiffre was hardly handsome: Mr. Big was positively frightening. Those yet to be described vary from the bland and sinister to the dreadful and grotesque. Drax, I think, is definitely the ugliest. In fact, the word 'ugly' becomes almost onomatopoeic where Sir Hugo is concerned. I nearly said that he *could* help his nature and attitude but *couldn't* help what he looked like. But I am reminded that he himself was responsible for the wartime explosion that kicked back at him and left his face only one of plastic surgery's partial successes. The hideous result, plus the knowledge that he engineered it himself, helped to twist the poor chap's mind. Starting off as a fanatical Nazi anyway, I don't think it surprising that he should develop a megalomania and a paranoia, after all he had gone through.

Drax gave the impression of being a little larger than life. He was physically big—about six foot tall, Bond guessed—and his shoulders were exceptionally broad. He had a big square head and the tight reddish hair was parted in the middle. On either side of the parting the hair dipped down in a curve towards the temples with the object, Bond assumed, of hiding as much as possible of the tissue of shining puckered skin that covered most of the right half of his face. Other relics of plastic surgery could be detected in the man's right ear, which was not a perfect match with its companion on the left, and the right eye, which had been a surgical failure. It was considerably larger than the left eye, because of a contraction of the borrowed skin used to rebuild the upper and lower eyelids, and it looked painfully bloodshot. Bond doubted if it was capable of closing completely, and he guessed that Drax covered it with a patch at night.

To conceal as much as possible of the unsightly taut

His Adversaries

skin that covered half his face, Drax had grown a bushy reddish moustache and had allowed his whiskers to grow down to the level of the lobes of his ears. He also had patches of hair on his cheek-bones.

That moustache also serves to camouflage a prognathous upper jaw that he was born with and a splaying of the teeth which Bond concludes came from his sucking of a thumb in his childhood. The general effect, observed by Bond and described by Fleming as being 'flamboyant', can only emphasize the paucity of mere words to give a true picture of this ogre.

Sir Hugo Drax gets beaten at the card table, of course, and Bond makes himself a packet, incidentally—£15,000, to be exact. This is a mere flea-bite to a multi-millionaire, but it's a very great deal to a civil servant. 'I should spend the money quickly, Commander Bond,' Drax advises him, somewhat ominously, and the fortunate winner decides to take the advice. He's all set for a really big spending spree the very next day, but before he can purchase or order a single thing Bond gets roped into the biggest adventure of his career to date. Drax, it develops, isn't only nasty: he's a wrong 'un, too. The highly-publicized launching of his Moonraker, supposedly directed on to a target eighty miles out into the North Sea, from the Dover district, is to be the culmination of a precise plan—a dastardly practical joke of such proportions that I humbly doff my castor in the direction of the author for his inventive and imaginative genius. Further elaboration might appear fulsome. Briefly, all the figures and settings apropos the aiming of the rocket have been altered ninety degrees to the left! The missile carries an atomic warhead, too. James Bond may have been a bit dim about wondering why Drax told him to 'spend the money quickly,' but let us thank the powers that be for such men in the Secret Service when the chips are down and the die is cast. I sleep a lot easier at night now I know that men like Bond are around.

James Bond hasn't—or at least he didn't have—a very great respect for American gangsters. 'They're not Americans. Mostly a lot of Italian bums with monogrammed shirts who spend the day eating spaghetti and meat-balls and squirting scent over themselves.'

He passes this opinion to the Chief of Staff early on in *Diamonds are Forever*. Now, Bond ought to know what he's talking about. It isn't as if he had based his ideas simply upon someone like Edgar Wallace's Tony Perelli, and it must be remembered that he speaks in the middle 'fifties: the spate of Warner Bros. revivals on television was still yet to come. No, Bond is an experienced Secret Service agent whose assignments have given him a pretty good insight into the worth of big-time criminals. His encounters with a varied trio of wrong-doers are fully documented up to this point—and they include *one* American gangster who gave him a rather rough time. He is not the type of man to generalize or to underestimate an opponent. I submit that Bond knows whereof he speaks.

But—'That's what you think,' says the Chief of Staff. He proceeds, in a single paragraph, to give Bond a brief summary of organized American crime in a manner so succinct and knowledgeable as to suggest that the night before he had been reading *Murder Inc.*, or one of the similar factual books that followed in its wake. He finishes: 'You're going to take those gangs on. And you'll be by yourself. Satisfied?'

Who on earth does he think he's talking to? Some jumped-up, tin-pot hoodlum with delusions of grandeur, intent upon muscling in on the big boy's territory? Has he forgotten that he is addressing the man who has crossed swords with SMERSH, the mind that out-manoeuvred Mr. Big, the spoke in the wheel of Sir Hugo Drax?

Bond's face relaxed. 'Come on, Bill,' he said. 'If that's all there is to it, I'll buy you lunch. It's my turn and I feel like celebrating . . . I'll take you to Scotts' and we'll have some of their dressed crab and a pint of black velvet. You've taken a load off my mind. I thought there might be some ghastly snag about this job.'

Cocky, complacent, over-confident? Is he riding for a fall? The tone of these early pages certainly suggest that James Bond is tending to underrate the diamond smugglers he has been briefed by M to foil, and that he is in for a nasty jolt. It follows, I think, that Ian Fleming holds pretty high cards. The implications are that Bond is going to have no cakewalk during this particular exploit. Now Fleming knows more than a bit about the subject of this book—he followed it up the next year with a 'documentary' called *The Diamond Smugglers*—and it is quite obvious that he is familiar with locales like the Jamaica race-track, in upper state New York, and with the casinos of Las Vegas, where much of the action takes place. He also knows that American gangsters are not spaghetti-eating Italians and very little more. I think that it was his intention to show the Spangled Mob as an extremely powerful underworld organization and its leaders as ruthless and frightening criminals, and with James Bond finally aware

His Adversaries

of a healthy respect for these top-notch hoodlums of the new world.

I don't think Ian Fleming has ever failed to give us an enthralling and exciting story, but in my opinion he came nearer to failing in this objective in *Diamonds are Forever* than in almost any other of his books. With the best will in the world I can't take Jack Spang and his brother, Seraffimo Spang, very seriously. They are extremely tough guys indeed, admittedly, but little more than that. Compared with most of the other villains there seems to me to be little about them that is frightening, dreadful or sinister. There *is* the mysterious telephone voice, of course, that of A B C, whose initials in phonetic French, lead to one Rufus B. Saye, but this is just an amusing gimmick. We had guessed that they might be one and the same all along, without having the savvy to realize why.

Says Felix Leiter: '... these Spangled boys are the tops. They've got a good machine, even if they do care to have funny names.' But it isn't only funny names: Seraffimo has funny hobbies. ' "He's daft,"* said the driver. "He's crazy about the Old West. Bought himself a whole ghost town way out on Highway 95. He's shored the place up—wooden sidewalks, a fancy saloon, clapboard hotel where he rooms the boys, even the old railway station." ' But Seraffimo Spang doesn't only play cowboys: he plays trains as well. He makes so much money out of his gambling joint on the 'Rue de la Pay' of Las Vegas that he spends it on extravagant toys like an old Western locomotive and one of the first Pullman state coaches, and he has riotous weekends, driving the train himself. 'Champagne and caviar, orchestra, girls—the works.' It sounds to me like a richman's *Genevieve* set-up, minus Kenneth More but plus about a dozen Kay Kendalls, and with Brighton replaced by Las Vegas.

Mr. Spang was dressed in full Western costume down to the long silver spurs on his polished black boots. The costume, and the broad leather chaps that covered his legs were in black, picked and embellished with silver. The big, quiet hands rested on the ivory butts of two long-barrelled revolvers which protruded from a holster down each thigh, and the broad black belt from which they hung was ribbed with ammunition.

Wyatt Earp? William S. Hart? Paladin? Fleming tells us that he should have looked ridiculous, but that he didn't. He

* Few American taxi-drivers would use such an expression, I feel. 'Daffy', yes; 'daft', no.

does to me, I'm afraid, but then I'm not in James Bond's situation when he is faced by this retarded adolescent.

Far, far more sinister than the Spang brothers, I think, are a couple of subsidiary characters: those two hired torpedoes from Detroit, Wint and Kidd, who move ominously and threateningly through the book. Cold and dispassionate mercenaries, they are direct descendants of Hemingway's 'The Killers'. One is 'youngish, with a pretty white face' and hair that is prematurely white. The other is fattish, and his face has 'the glistening, pasty appearance of a spat-out bullseye.' Their looks and their demeanour, together with the suggestion of a homosexual relationship between them—(Fleming's intention or merely my assumption?)—make me feel like shuddering.* The Spang boys make me feel like smiling.

Among James Bond's many adversaries, we remember this one for his frightening looks, that one for his excessive sadism, and the other because he's so smooth and unflappable. They are *all* pretty calm and unruffled, I suppose, each one has a nice line in torture and rather enjoys putting it into practice, and not a man jack among them is exactly what you would call prepossessing in appearance. All in all, they are a very unpleasant bunch. Of the lot, I think that Col. Rosa Klebb is the most unpleasant of all—whichever way you take her. Or should I say *it?* Strictly speaking, I suppose Col. Klebb is female, and should be designated by the appropriate gender. But any resemblance she bears to femininity or femineity is purely accidental.

Rosa appears in *From Russia, With Love*. She is the Head of Otdyel II, the department of SMERSH in charge of Operations and Executions, and Ian Fleming surpasses himself with the character he draws for this nastiest of all nasty females. Kronsteen, champion chess-player of Moscow, sums her up as a Neuter. She is neither heterosexual nor homosexual, and although he decides that she 'might enjoy the act physically,' the instrument of her enjoyment is of no importance to her. For Rosa Klebb, 'sex was nothing more than an itch.' Kronsteen, whom Fleming calls the Wizard of Ice, and who is utterly unemotional, appears to have no feelings one way or the other about her as a person or a human being, and yet he does seem to envy her. She has something which he hasn't, and which he sees as an advantage and a quality. 'Sexual neutrality was the essence of coldness in an individual. It was a great and wonderful thing to be born with.' It is this total lack of normal human emotions which has been such a

---

* Homosexuals please note: nothing snide, snotty or personal intended here. You would shudder at Wint and Kidd, too.

His Adversaries

help to Rosa Klebb in becoming one of the most powerful women in Soviet Russia.

She was glamorized like hell when they made the film: this was unavoidable. Casting must have been a nightmare. Lotte Lenya, the lady chosen to portray her, was excellent—within the limits of the script. This had to be tailored to suit conditions: all the improved cinematic techniques of recent years have never equalled an author's word-magic and a reader's imagination. They never will.

Rosa looks like a toad. She is middle-aged, short and dumpy. 'The devil knows, thought Kronsteen, what her breasts were like, but the bulge of uniform that rested on the table-top looked like a badly packed sandbag, and in general her figure, with its big pear-shaped hips, could only be likened to a 'cello.'

Her face is worse, and her observer is reminded of the *tricoteuses* of the French Revolution. They must have been a pretty horrible lot if they were anything like Rosa to look at, what with her 'thinning orange hair scraped back to the tight, obscene bun ... the wedge of thickly powdered, large-pored nose; the wet trap of a mouth ... pale, thick chicken's skin that scragged in little folds under the eyes and at the corners of the mouth ... big peasant's ears ...' Ugh. On top of all this, Rosa doesn't wash very often, and she stinks.

The foregoing is merely an abbreviation of her appearance as seen by one man: Kronsteen. It picks out the salient features of this horrible-looking little woman. But she hasn't got a beautiful nature to compensate. Her disposition, if anything, is worse than her looks. It is said in Moscow that she allows no torturing to take place unless she is present, and it is this revolting monster who is in charge of a well-planned *konspiratsia* to destroy James Bond.

It may be recalled that the delightful Tatiana Romanova is in on this conspiracy, too. She receives an imperious summons to Rosa's room, some six floors up in the barracks where they both abide. The poor girl nearly dies of fright at the prospect of having to face 'the central horror' of the dreaded and literally unspeakable SMERSH. 'The very name of the organization was abhorred and avoided ... It was an obscene word, a word from the tomb, the very whisper of death ...'

But once ensconced with the toad in its hole, things begin to look a little bit different to Tania, particularly when she learns that she isn't to be punished for the only crime she can remember having committed: stealing a spoon. Briefed by Rosa Klebb for her part in the plan against Bond, although she isn't given the *full* dastardly gem, Tania begins to feel quite important and excited about it all. She is left to think it all over while Rosa retires into the next room to 'tidy up'. It is at this point that Ian Fleming plays his master stroke in the characterization of Rosa Klebb. She reappears a little later, twirling on her toes and posing like a model. No wonder Tania's jaw drops.

> Colonel Rosa Klebb of SMERSH was wearing a semi-transparent nightgown in orange *crépe de chine*. It had scallops of the same material round the low square neckline and scallops at the wrists of the broadly flounced sleeves. Underneath could be seen a brassière consisting of two large pink satin roses. Below, she wore old-fashioned knickers of pink satin with elastic above the knees. One dimpled knee, like a yellowish coconut, appeared thrust forward between the half open folds of the nightgown in the classic stance of the modeller. The feet were enclosed in pink satin slippers with pompoms of ostrich feathers. Rosa Klebb had taken off her spectacles and her naked face was now thick with mascara and rouge and lipstick.
> She looked like the oldest and ugliest whore in the world.

I don't think it surprising that Tania's nerve should break and that she gets out of that room as fast as her legs can take her.

It has been said earlier that of all these deliciously absurd books, *From Russia, With Love* is the one that I like the best. Not only does it have my favourite heroine, Tatiana, it also has Rosa Klebb, the woman I love to hate. It has the best plot, in my opinion, and the best writing. Incidentally, the original edition has the best dust-jacket, too, and Richard Chopping hasn't done a bad one *yet*. Internally and externally, I think the book has much to commend it. Its atmosphere is wonderful: its pace—leisurely at first—compelling and *crescendo*. It positively overflows with delightful characters: herein May makes her bow. Then there's Darko Kerim—(what a throwaway!)—Tania herself, and the memorable Rosa. But even more memorable than Rosa, perhaps, is the book's other villain: Granitsky.

His real name is Donovan Grant. He 'was the result of a midnight union between a German professional weight-lifter and a Southern Irish waitress. The union lasted for a quarter of an hour on the damp grass behind a circus tent outside Belfast.' He's a bastard whichever way you look at him. We get quite a lot about his early life in the first few pages of

From Russia, With Love, and much about his appearance and character. It makes absorbing reading. He grows into a big strong lad in Northern Ireland, and he gets 'feelings' round about the time of the full moon. He starts off by strangling a cat, and then progresses to a big sheep-dog. Naturally, this is done clandestinely, and nocturnally. He cuts himself the throat of a cow, 'for Christmas'. It isn't long before he starts going in for the big stuff, and after accounting for a sleeping tramp one night he begins to kill 'the occasional girl'.

This sort of thing makes him feel good. Sex doesn't enter into the business: he can never understand what that's all about. When he takes up boxing and submits himself to a rigorous discipline in a Belfast gymnasium he nearly kills one of his sparring partners with his fists when the moon is full and he can't get out of the place.

After he has been called up for military service and is stationed in Berlin, it seems quite a logical progression that Grant should be attracted eastwards. 'He liked all he heard about the Russians, their brutality, their carelessness of human life, and their guile, and he decided to go over to them.'* He does, too. It isn't easy. I don't think it was easy, either, for Fleming to write about this man, and to tell us how, step by step, and by following orders without question, he convinces his new masters of how he likes killing and can become a very valuable man to them. Writing of this sort could quickly become ridiculous: Fleming has often been accused of extravagance. I don't think it is ridiculous here. I may be extremely gullible and credulous, of course, but I find I can believe every word of it. I think it is that well done. This past history of the former Donovan 'Red' Grant is offered to us in a sort of flashback, while he is travelling towards an appointment involving the Bond *konspiratsia*. He is now Krassno Granitski, and he has been so for the past ten years. His code-name is 'Granit'. He is the Chief Executioner of SMERSH.

James Bond does get 'em, doesn't he?

The trouble with trying to write about these villains is that, chronologically, with one or two exceptions, each one seems more villainous than the last.

Dr. No is without doubt the most sinister of the lot. He reminds me a great deal of the old devil doctor himself: Fu Manchu. He wasn't made to appear so in the film, and Joseph Wiseman played him strictly streamlined and nineteen-sixtyish. But Fleming's description in the book, compared

* When *that* was written Russia was deep in the doghouse. When *this* is written, it reads a bit strangely.

with what I remember of Sax Rohmer's famous character, give the two certain similarities. Dr. No is at least six inches taller than Bond, for a start, and Bond is pretty big. The doctor *seems* even taller than he really is. This is because of straightness and poise. 'The head was also elongated and tapered from a round, completely bald skull down to a sharp chin so that the impression was of a reversed raindrop—or rather oildrop, for the skin was of a deep almost translucent yellow.' A nice touch, that.

Dr. No is one of these ageless criminals. You know, the type who could be forty or a hundred and forty, like old Fu. He has no lines at all on his face, and then there's that bald, polished dome. He has eyebrows rather like Dali, but no eyelashes at all. He also wears a full-length kimono in gunmetal grey.

> The bizarre, gliding figure looked like a giant venomous worm wrapped in grey tin-foil, and Bond would not have been surprised to see the rest of it trailing, slimily along the carpet behind.

Dr. No is the acme of Oriental politeness, and he apologizes for not shaking hands. He hasn't got any. In their place he has two pairs of articulated steel pincers. He wears contact lenses, and on one occasion he raises a metal claw and taps the centres of his eyeballs, each of which 'in turn emitted a dull ting. "These," said Doctor No, "see everything."'

He has had a very interesting life. From an early age he had been closely connected with the Chinese Tongs. By the age of thirty he was the treasurer of the Hip Sings, one of the most powerful Tongs in the United States, and he was ambitious, too. He absconded with a million dollars in gold and went into hiding in New York's Harlem. But the Tong caught up with him. Its members tortured him all night to find out where he had hidden the gold. 'When they could not break me, they cut off my hands to show that the corpse was that of a thief, and they shot me through the heart and went away. But they did not know something about me. I am the one man in a million who has his heart on the right side of his body... I lived.'

Dr. No puts this down to sheer will-power. I put it down to sheer luck that somebody not very far away happened in on his Harlem hideout almost immediately after the visitors had left. After you've had a night of torture, the shock to your system of being subjected to the rough amputation of both hands without anaesthetic must be considerable. In this state, and obviously bleeding to death from at least two sources, a bullet through the chest at close range—whether

His Adversaries

your heart is on the left, on the right, or in your mouth—isn't going to help matters. Dr. No may be justified in claiming that his will was the power that brought him through the subsequent operation and months of hospitalization, but he *should* have paid passing acknowledgment to some off-stage Harlem humanitarian who kept himself to himself during those night-long torture screams, if there was any, but who very quickly investigated and telephoned a hospital after he heard the shot and the retreating patter of Chinese feet.

But Dr. No didn't slip up a second time. Once he had more or less recovered, he invested much of his million in just one envelope of rare postage stamps. Meanwhile, he changed his appearance. Among other things, he had all his hair removed by the roots! 'I could not get smaller, so I made myself taller. I wore built up shoes. I had weeks of traction on my spine...I threw away my spectacles and wore contact lenses—one of the first pairs ever built.' Then, with a new name, he went to Milwaukee, where there are no Chinese, and buried himself in the academic world. He studied the human mind and body.... Why? Because I wished to know what this clay is capable of. I had to learn what my tools were before I put them to use on my next goal—total security from physical weaknesses, from material dangers and from the hazards of living. Then, Mr. Bond, from the secure base, armed even against the casual slings and arrows of the world, I would proceed to the achievement of power—the power, Mr. Bond, to do unto others what had been done unto me, the power of life and death, the power to decide, to judge, the power of absolute independence from outside authority.

His secure base is a private island off Jamaica. Deep in the heart of a mountain he has built himself a sort of underground Shangri La, but one far more palatial than that earthly paradise. As a very profitable cover for his main activities he runs a thriving business in guano: bird dung—an excellent fertilizer. His workers, all loyal to the last man, scared stiff of his very name and each, apparently, as wicked as sin, make millions for the doctor. The average wage among them seems to be twelve bob a week, some twenty percent more than they could get back on the mainland. The overseers get a pound. The overheads are negligible: Dr. No doesn't have to pay the birds anything at all. 'Each one is a simple factory for turning fish into dung. The digging of the guano is only a question of not spoiling the crop by digging too much.' There is plenty of the stuff, he has a never-ending demand for it, and the whole business is almost entirely profit.

If there were nothing more to Dr. No than his guano operation it would be reasonable to conclude that he is very little worse than the operator of a sweat-shop.

But he's stark, raving mad, too, of course—as if you hadn't guessed. On the face of things he has voluntarily entombed himself in a luxurious fortress and is merely the king of a very small dung heap indeed. As Bond informs him, it's the old delusion of grandeur. The asylums are full of people like Dr. No. 'The only difference is that instead of being shut up, you've built your own asylum and shut yourself up in it.'

There is some method in the man's madness, though. Dr. No isn't a drooling lunatic. Guano merely finances his primary operation, that of sabotaging American guided missile tests a few hundred miles away. Not unexpectedly, we learn that he's in cohorts with Russia in this venture, and there is a million dollar's worth of scientific equipment installed up there on the mountain. There is nothing ideological about the scheme: the profit motive is Dr. No's main concern. Already he has his eye on Communist China, who may be prepared to pay him even more than Russia.

When this book was written the cold war was very cold. By the time the film of the book was made things had warmed up considerably, and it would hardly have been polite, to say the least, to accuse a friendly power like Russia of financing such a project. On the screen, you will find that the Russian Government had nothing to do with it. Here, Dr. No works for that sinister organization called SPECTRE—one devoted purely to private enterprise.

As something of a hobby, this fascinating gentleman likes to hurt people, just to see how much pain they can stand. He emphatically discourages visitors to his island, but trespassers—and those among his workers who have to be punished—serve as his guinea-pigs. He's just a great big benefactor to the human race, really. His captives, Bond and Honeychile Rider, are to do *their* bit for humanity: 'You have both put me to a great deal of trouble. In exchange I intend to put you to a great deal of pain. I shall record the length of your endurance. The facts will be noted. One day my findings will be given to the world. Your deaths will have served the purposes of science. I never waste human material.'

All very well. He can chat like this *now*, with the pair of them a couple of flies in his web. Earlier on he had made at least two attempts to eliminate Bond back in Jamaica, and before the Secret Service agent had ever come *near* the island. The first shot, injecting a nectarine with poison, had misfired completely. The second, arranging to have a six-inch-long centipede—also poison—put into Bond's hotel bed, came rather nearer to scoring a bull. I rate the three or so pages describing this minor adventure as the outstanding highlight of Ian Fleming's efforts among episodes of suspense.

What with a flame-thrower, man-eating crabs and a giant squid fifty feet long, Dr. No certainly enlists some horrifying allies during the course of this book. But he dies a very unpleasant death himself. It seems to me to be both a rough and poetic justice that one who lives by guano should also perish by it, too. But whatever happened to all those twelve-bob-a-week diggers?

Auric Goldfinger stands about five feet high, and so much of him is out of proportion that he looks as though he has been put together with pieces of other people's bodies. He has a moon-shaped face and an enormous round head. Everything about him is either golden or reddish-yellow: his name, his sun-tanned skin, the carroty hair on his head and the orange hair on his chest. Even the car he runs is a bright yellow. He is one of the richest men in the world and he keeps much of his wealth in gold bars. He possesses more than he could ever possibly need, but it still isn't enough for Goldfinger. Simply, he just loves the stuff. Even the girls he buys for himself have to be painted golden. He wants to be the richest man in history and he sets himself a pretty hard task in order to fulfil this ambition. One sometimes hears a very apt remark from Americans, when they are referring to a seemingly impossible feat: 'it would be like trying to rob Fort Knox.' Goldfinger attempts exactly that!

This character looks ludicrous, he thinks like a paranoiac, and he plans a scheme which, at first glance, is utterly farfetched. All this *should* add up to one of the most laughably ridiculous books ever published. I have no doubt that there are a few people who think it is. Millions of others don't: they read it absorbingly and recommend it strongly to those who haven't. It is one of Fleming's more popular efforts among a near dozen, not one of which has proved to be exactly unpopular. This is despite its many extravagancies of invention and imagination.

Ian Fleming walked an extremely shaky tight-rope across a pond of very thin ice when he wrote *Goldfinger*. It is only that the mixing of my metaphors might become *too* maladroit that I hesitate to say outright that he eventually came down firmly on both feet. But you know what I mean, I'm sure.

Not that *Goldfinger* did not lay itself open to parody. As

a matter of fact it inspired two Harvard undergraduates to lampoon the whole Fleming output hilariously in an all too slim little effort entitled *Alligator*. This book, reviewed in England at a moment when it was virtually unobtainable, caused much frustration among potential readers when they could not buy it and among booksellers when they could not supply it. Lacertus Alligator has a head like a football, steel teeth and very bad manners: he is a sort of composite Mr. Big, Dr. No and Hugo Drax. He stands no more than four feet eleven, wears a purple suit with a mauve and violet shirt and tie, and his face is covered with a tiny network of purple veins. He also insists on his girl being clothed in similar colours and carries a small aerosol can containing a vegetable dye. He sprays everyone he encounters purple. He also kidnaps the Queen, the Prime Minister and the Cabinet, among others, and he steals the Houses of Parliament by undermining them and floating them down the Thames to the sea, having earlier blown up all the bridges in his way! It is a riotous pastiche brilliantly written in the Ian Fleming manner and was undoubtedly inspired primarily by *Goldfinger*.

Difficult to accept though Auric Goldfinger and his ambitions and activities may be, the book in which he figures is one of the most entertaining pieces of hokum ever penned. Fleming, who had earlier held us spellbound with a lengthy game of baccarat, a nine-page meal and then eighteen pages of bridge, here surpasses himself. He devotes no less than two chapters—thirty-three pages—to a game of golf between Goldfinger and Bond. I, for one, would not have had this particular game shortened by a single line, although I do not play golf and have never understood the compulsive hold it has on so many people. On reflection, I find that cards ordinarily bore me stiff, and I have a delicate stomach. Further, I have never driven a car in my life and could not set one into motion in the direst emergency—the delights of driving and the description of vehicles being another of the preoccupations in this and other books of Fleming's. I can only humbly conclude that I am under the spell of a master when I become absorbed by passages dealing with pastimes and occupations with which I would normally have not the slightest concern. A healthy interest in the more personable members of the opposite sex is, in fact, just about the only thing I have in common with James Bond or any of his adversaries.

Goldfinger groups some pretty tough guys about him during the course of the narrative. Never very far away from

His Adversaries

him is his chauffeur-bodyguard, a huge Korean whom he calls Oddjob. This frightening brute has a cleft palate and his conversation is limited to utterances like 'Oargn,' and 'Garch a har?' Goldfinger is the only one who can understand him. The second remark is as near to 'Coat and hat?' as he can get. I never did figure out exactly what the other one means. Oddjob has ridges of bonelike tissue down the edge of each of his big hands, and just as a demonstration of his prowess he splits a six by four polished oak banister in two with a couple of axelike chops with one hand. Had this book been written only a year or two earlier the idea of a man with a couple of built-in choppers at the end of his arms would have appeared too farfetched even for *this* book. But we have learned a lot about the art of Karate since then. As Goldfinger says: 'Karate is a branch of judo, but it is to judo what a Spandau is to a catapult.' Oddjob may be just a *little* larger than life and possibly oaken rails of six by four is laying it on a bit too thick, as it were, but similar things *can* be done with the naked hand. I have seen them done, and it is frightening. The idea of men even remotely like Oddjob wandering loose in the world is positively terrifying.

I find it strange that creatures like Oddjob and his grotesque employer should be quite acceptable to me and yet the big-time American gang leaders who put in an appearance late in the book should seem far more like caricatures than anything else. I am reminded of the Spangled Mob, back in *Diamonds are Forever*. In fact, that particular gang is again represented here. The descriptions of them all are credible enough, I suppose: I think it must be my sensitivity to names which makes them all so ridiculous to me. I know that there *were* real people called Jack 'Legs' Diamond, 'Baby-Face' Nelson and 'Pretty Boy' Floyd, and that they were very hard guys indeed. But Fleming's fictional Jed Midnight, Billy (The Grinner) Ring, Jack Strap and Mr. Solo appear to me to be trying too hard to be tough. In Max Eastman's famous words, they have false hair on their chests. As a wrong 'un, even the delightful Miss Pussy Galore is only just acceptable.

What with its characters and its situations, *Goldfinger* is perhaps the most bizarre example in a generally somewhat extraordinary output. But it is also, I submit, at the same time one of the best.

I am sorry to have to keep harping on this business of Bond's American adversaries. With *The Spy Who Loved Me* I'll try to keep it short.

The two thugs who form the opposition here are just

thugs and nothing more. No arch-criminals this time, no masterminds. Just a couple of hired gunmen straight out of James Hadley Chase. The leader is called Sol Horowitz: Horror for short—'a frightening lizard of a man'. His minion is Sluggsy Morant. He looks 'a young monster, the sort that pulls wings off flies'. Compared with people like Mr. Big and Goldfinger, they might almost be light relief, if it were not for the fact that they are so frighteningly unpleasant.

Once again, with the best will in the world, I can't take them very seriously. Although there are few English writers able to handle the American idiom, vernacular and slang as well as Ian Fleming, I find the dialogue spoken by this precious pair almost embarrassingly overdone. For instance, this is Mr. Morant appraising Vivienne Michel: ' "Say, Horror," he winked at the other man. "This is some bimbo! Git an eyeful of those knockers! And a rear-end to match! Geez, what a dish!" ' Horror is not much different: 'The thin man gave a short, barking laugh. "Ixnay, Sluggsy. I said later. Leave the stupid slot be. There's all night for that. Git goin' like I said." '

These are mild exchanges compared with some. Now Fleming is just as popular in the States as he is in England, so presumably this sort of thing is not too much off-key, if at all. Perhaps it just seems to *me* that it is exaggerated. I have seen no American reviews of the book, so I can't say how Sluggsy and Horror went down over there. But it certainly does read to me, an Englishman, as similar dialogue written by an American might appear: 'Gorblimey, 'Orror, me ol' mate. This bleedin' cow's quite a heyeful, hain't she? Take a butcher's at them there Archie Pitts!' Etc. etc.

Still, no matter how they sound, or even how they act, these two hoodlums are professionals, and when James Bond interferes with their nefarious undertakings they set out to take care of him. Poor little small-time crooks. How could they know whom they were facing? Bond could wipe out cruds of their character and hardly raise a sweat. He would have done, too, but for Viv mucking things up a little. She just makes the job a little bit harder, that's all.

Ernst Stavro Blofeld is one of the most engaging criminals in sensational fiction. He bids fair to rival villains like Carl Peterson and Professor Moriarty.

He was born in Gdynia. His father was Polish and his mother was Greek. In passing, it might be added that his birthday, 28 May, 1908, is the same as Ian Fleming's. In his early days he travelled to Sweden, Turkey and South America, after having juggled with stolen funds which, suitably invested, eventually left him quite wealthy. But riches aren't enough for Blofeld: they never are with these kinky characters.

Commencing his career of crime proper, he finally settles in Paris. His centre of operations is camouflaged behind a brass plate in the Boulevard Haussman, which says: *F.I.R.C.O.* These initials stand for the *Fratérnite Internationale de la Résistance Contre l'Oppression.*

His criminal organization is large. The twenty men who make up his executive at the time we first learn about him are a cosmopolitan lot, consisting of cells of three from six national groups, plus an East German physicist and a Polish electronics expert. The six national groups are Sicilian, Corsican, French, Russian, German, Yugoslavian and Turkish. Which common language—or languages—they speak when they are all together we are not told. Considering the nationalities involved, it would seem doubtful that it is English. Yet, strangely enough, the real name of this organization is an English one! It is The Special Executive for Counterintelligence, Terrorism, Revenge and Extortion. Why Blofeld chose English for the name of this enterprise is almost immediately obvious: it contracts down to a nice, sinister abbreviation— SPECTRE. But it also forms a word not *particularly* English. A spectre's a spectre in plenty of other European countries, too.

Blofeld's a paranoiac, naturally. He *must* be. How else can one explain a wealthy man who, having only recently kidnapped a seventeen-year-old girl and having successfully demanded one million dollars ransom from her father, chooses not to rest on his laurels but cooks up something infinitely bigger only a few weeks later?

Of course, that million-dollar operation *had* been upset just a trifle. Blofeld had said that on receipt of the ransom the girl would be returned unharmed. But she wasn't. She was Carnally Known. Whether she was violated, as her parents maintain, or whether she consented, is neither here nor there. Blofeld is not one to split hairs.

... We are a large and very powerful organization. I am not concerned with morals or ethics, but members will be aware that I desire, and most strongly recommend, that SPECTRE shall conduct itself in a superior fashion. There is no discipline in SPECTRE except self-discipline. We are a dedicated fraternity whose strength lies entirely in the strength of each member. Weakness in one member is the death-watch beetle in the total structure. You are aware of my views in this matter, and on the occasion when cleansing has been necessary you have approved my action. In this case I have already done what I considered necessary vis-à-vis this girl's family. I have returned half a million dollars with an appropriate note of apology.

Retribution for the wrong-doer follows hard upon the heels of this homily. Then—back to the job in hand.

Blofeld's newest essay into big business is on a much grander scale, although he follows a well-worn and profitable path. It's kidnapping of a sort again, perhaps, but this time no girls are involved. The hostages on this occasion are a couple of atomic bombs, and the ransom demanded is one hundred million *pounds*. This is pretty reasonable when you consider the probabilities if ever these two bombs are detonated. The doting daddies—this time the Prime Minister of Great Britain and the President of the United States—are in a bit of a tizzy.

Badly outlined here, prognosticated in *précis,* the whole thing seems a bit far-fetched. It isn't, really. If you haven't already read *Thunderball*, do so. You'll see why.

We don't get a lot of Blofeld in this book. He's a cunning sort of chap, inclined to delegate all the dirty work to expendable underlings. When Bond has saved the world and has roped in quite a few of SPECTRE's top men, 'a bunch of bigtime hoodlums—ex-operators of SMERSH, the Mafia, the Gestapo—all the big outfits,' there is no Blofeld. He eludes the net. I don't think many readers minded at the time. It seemed certain that he would turn up again. He does, too.

Blofeld puts in a second appearance in *On Her Majesty's Secret Service*. By this time he has built up his organization again, and now he has forsaken nuclear weapons for an idea that makes mere germ warfare look like a game with bows and arrows. Fowl Pest, Colorado beetle, Swine Fever and anthrax are only a few of his allies. He is directing his operation against Britain, too. And he doesn't need anyone else to finance him. He can manage entirely on his own. 'All he has to do is go a bear of sterling and Gilt-Edged.'

Bond has the ball. It's up to him, and he's confident. 'Only *he* could do the cleaning up. It was written in his stars!'

That Blofeld is a master of disguise second to not even Carl Peterson is now undeniable. Bond had never even had a glimpse of him all through the *Thunderball* operation, and only had written descriptions to go by later on, but *we* know exactly what he looked like then. He weighed twenty stone,

His Adversaries

for a start, with a great big belly. When Bond first meets him, in *this* book, he isn't more than twelve stone, and the fact that he is conveniently clothed in hardly more than a woollen loin slip suggests that he might even be the wrong man, 'for there were no signs of the sagging flesh that comes from middle-aged weight reduction.' Whereas in *Thunderball* he had a 'large, white, bland face under the wiry black crew cut', he now has 'longish, carefully-tended, almost dandified hair that was a fine silvery white.' Cunning devil! Anyone can change the style of his hair, of course, and even its length, but it takes a Blofeld to alter his from wiry to fine. And although the mouth had once been 'proud and thin, like a badly healed wound', with 'compressed, dark lips capable only of false, ugly smiles', things are very different now. Blofeld's mouth is 'full and friendly, with a pleasant, upturned, but perhaps rather unwavering smile.' He can't disguise his height, though, or even the long and thin hands and feet. Surgery could have been responsible for removing the heavy lobes from his ears—and it obviously was—but what about those eyes? No changing *them*. They had been 'deep black pools surrounded—totally surrounded, as Mussolini's were—by very clear whites.' Now they are 'only rather frightening dark-green pools.' He wears tinted contact lenses.

Blofeld's *pièce de résistance* in this matter of adopting a disguise and adopting a new personality undoubtedly concerns his nose. It *had* been heavy and squat. Now it is aquiline, and his right nostril is 'eaten away, poor chap, by what looked like the badge of tertiary syphilis.' This touch *couldn't* be genuine, could it? After all, in *Thunderball*, 'he had never been known to sleep with a member of either sex.' He couldn't have caught a dose that way... Congenital syphilis would have shown up years before... Ah—perhaps he caught it from a lavatory seat?

But the main thing that eludes me about the new Blofeld is why he should have gone to all this trouble about changing his physical appearance, even to a nostril eaten away by venereal disease, real or false, and to the texture of his hair, probably a wig—either of which possible subterfuges could have been determined by a not too close official inspection—and then, out of nothing more or less than vanity, that he should blow the whole gaff. Calling himself the Comte de Bleuville, and determined to establish his right to the title, he swallows hook, line *and* sinker. In genealogical pursuit, he admits to Bond that his father's name was Ernst George Blofeld and his mother's Maria Stavro Michelopoulos. I am well aware that if he hadn't we would have had no story, no *On Her Majesty's Secret Service*.

At the time of writing, Blofeld is still at large. Bond is sure to get him in the end: there's no doubt about that. It's just a matter of time. Whether Blofeld will continue to do a Fu Manchu act at the end of many books to come and somehow elude the net, or whether he will only last a few rounds, as did Carl Peterson, time alone will tell. But James Bond has got a particular score to settle with Ernst Stavro Blofeld, and when the day of reckoning comes it is going to make interesting reading.

His Future

THE ACTIVE CAREER of Sherlock Holmes extended for nearly forty years, with a little time out when he went over the Reichenbach Falls with Moriarty, ostensibly in a struggle to the death. He came back none the worse for this experience and carried on until he was past retirement age. Someone, I don't know who, made the now famous remark: 'He may not have been killed when he went over the cliff, but he was never quite the same man afterwards.'

Conan Doyle was as amused by this criticism as the rest of us, but he didn't agree with it. Prefacing the omnibus edition of the stories in 1928 he argued that as Holmes' methods and character became more familiar to his readers so the element of surprise grew less, and that the later tales suffered by comparison. In presenting them all in one volume, with the reader able to dip into them wherever he wanted to, Doyle hoped that there was no conspicuous falling off apparent in the quality of the stories towards the end.

There *isn't* a great deal of difference to speak of. Naturally, the hansom-cab atmosphere of London in the 'eighties and 'nineties could not be maintained into the nineteen-twenties and the jazz age, but as Holmes was fond of saying, 'You know my methods, Watson.' Those methods didn't change and his character remained the same, with only minor differences.

Criticism of this sort is inevitable, I suppose, with any popular figure in fiction who endures from tale to tale and from book to book. His readers get used to him and they grow fond of him, and they resent it if he doesn't appear to act as they expect him to. A character like Soames Forsyte,

His Future

of course, is quite a different matter. Galsworthy, in another *genre*, gives us the portrait of this man over a period of some forty-five years, and we watch him grow older, change almost imperceptibly and mellow with the passing of time. Compare the reserved and unsympathetic young Soames of *The Man of Property* with the likeable old chap of *Swan Song*.

But let us stick to 'light' fiction, and eschew that more commonly termed 'serious'. Among the popular characters, James Bond has, quite naturally, suffered from the sort of censure I am talking about even during his comparatively short career. Or rather, Ian Fleming has. Each new book, as it comes out, finds a few reviewers complaining that it isn't a patch on the earlier ones. Most of their criticism seems to revolve about the charge that Bond's latest exploit is altogether too outrageous. They tell us that Fleming has overstepped the mark and that his stuff is now too fantastic. Parallel with this sort of criticism is that of 'the mixture as before' school.

Once you're in the Fleming class you just can't win, with some reviewers, whatever you do. I don't suppose Fleming minds very much: fortunately there are those other critics who accept the books for what they are and who render an entirely different judgment. The books all sell, anyway. They would still sell if no papers or journals ever noticed them. It has long been accepted in the publishing trade that sales have never necessarily depended upon good reviews or even extensive newspaper advertising. The public grape-vine and the asphalt-jungle telegraph, if they don't do *all* that is needed, do a very great deal.

James Bond is set for life, or at least for as long as Ian Fleming cares to keep him going. The autumn of 1963 proved this, if nothing else did. October saw the release of the film version of *From Russia, With Love,* and it broke all box-office records. I think it is an interesting point, and well worth mentioning, that I happened to spend the whole of this month in hospital. Confined to my insular little world for some thirty days, it was absorbing to watch the development of events over that period. Bored to death by the necessarily stultifying existence of the ward's confines, several fellow-patients flapped and gasped, almost literally, like fishes out of water. *Daily Mirror* read, doctor's visit passed, the rest of the day stretched ahead with only the tell-tale trundle of trolleys and the tinkle of tin against tea-cups to relieve the monotony of the convalescent's life. Conversation was not a lost art: it had never been found. Light and Home were both woolly and vociferous. Television had not, as yet, penetrated these dark and uncharted regions. The mobile library, twice a week, offered brief succour as it passed, but what to choose? What tantalizing title or decorative dust-jacket to select, somewhat apprehensively, until next time round?

I saw certain Fleming works. I recommended them strongly. Either my enthusiasm was infectious or else my fellow-patients, already conditioned to accepting 'doctor's orders', were bludgeoned by an air of authority. The available books were devoured hungrily and exchanged impatiently. The fortuitous and quite coincidental reviews of the film of *From Russia, With Love* in the daily and evening newspapers fanned the flames. A certain Nurse Bond, comely and communicative, became both the butt and the envy of the ward: on her evening off she had excursed as far as Victoria—a mere half mile away—and had seen the film!

What did it matter that front-page headlines told us that Macmillan was in *our* position: incarcerated and under the knife? Of what importance was this Hailsham-Hogg and Home-Hume Business? Who made the better reading: Butler or Bond?

I relate this personal observation as just one illustration of the sort of thing that was going on, in some way or another, all over the country in October. Everyone suddenly seemed to be Bond-conscious. The booksellers' *Trade News* had this to say a week or two later:

> Jubilant PAN have voiced what most people must have realized by now—that 'British publishing has never known anything quite like James Bond'. Need we tell you, he continues to turn up in our newspapers and magazines, to dominate bookshop paper-back displays, and fill cinemas. Sales meanwhile go up and up, bringing delight to Mr. Fleming, his publishers *and* to booksellers everywhere.
>
> Hard facts. Although only five British paper-backs have so far hit that magic million-sale, two Flemings are due shortly to join this elite list. They are, as you will have guessed, *Dr. No* and *From Russia, With Love*.
>
> Just for the record, whilst the latter sold 183,000 in October alone, total sales of James Bond sagas for the same month were 733,700.
>
> If that weren't enough, PAN have computed that so far this year more than four million James Bonds have been sold. And by Christmas they predict that the figure will be near on five million.
>
> The jubilation is certainly understandable.

These books seem to appeal to all classes and to all types

of mind. I never cease to be surprised at the wide variety of people who read Fleming. For instance, during that recent High Court case involving a matter of copyright, counsel representing the plaintiff was describing Bond: 'An undercover agent in the British Secret Service—tough, hard-hitting, hard-drinking, hard-living and amoral, who at regular intervals saves the citizens of this country and the whole free world from the most incredible disasters.'

'Yes,' commented the learned judge drily, 'I have been saved myself.'

Again, when I was in the early stages of preparing this book, there came to my notice the review of that brilliant parody of Ian Fleming, published in the States but apparently unobtainable in this country. I knew little about it, but I could not afford to ignore it if it might have some bearing on what I was doing. Obtaining it speedily was of the utmost importance, so I wrote to an acquaintance of mine in New York, a bibliophile and an editor of some distinction, whom I knew would do his best to help me quickly. It did not occur to me that he might know anything at all about *Alligator* or even the James Bond books. Bibliographical scholarship, while often going hand in hand with the more abstruse who-dun-its, does not normally embrace the lusty thriller. I now blush at the thought of my detailed directions to one whom I imagined would be in strange territory. His reply was surprising.

> I have always been an admirer of Mr. Ian Fleming—after all he *is* the angel who subsidizes that elegant quarterly of the book world, *The Book Collector*. The parody of his more outlandish performances is, to me, so entertaining that I have had suspicions about Mr. Fleming himself doing some of it. At any rate, I purchased, and gave away, more than a dozen copies of *Alligator* in the past year. I am sending you, with best wishes, the only copy I have left on my shelves.

One sees in the gossip columns that the Duke of Edinburgh reads Fleming avidly. We are told, too, that each new Bond book used to be flown out to President Kennedy the moment it was published. Whether this be true or not it is an ironical fact that during police investigations Lee Oswald was discovered to have borrowed several of these books from the Dallas Public Library.

Both Bond and Fleming appear to be fair game—even fairground game. Each has played the part of Aunt Sally for some time. In addition, neither escaped the barbs during that satirical salvo for which the year 1963 will, among so many other things, be remembered. Both television's 'That Was The Week That Was' and journalism's *Private Eye* pricked and jabbed them lightly and amusingly. In a different league entirely, Cyril Connolly gave us 'Bond Strikes Camp', while a little earlier the 'Harvard Lampoon' had published the aforementioned *Alligator*, surely one of the most polished things of its kind ever done.

Of non-constructive criticism of the pair there has been plenty, in review, essay and conversation. I confess to a carping tongue and a certain captiousness myself—though I love them both to death, really. I also claim an interest in, and a captivation by all these yarns and characters with an absorption so complete that it becomes almost proprietary. I feel entitled to administer the gentle rebuke, no matter how wrong I might really be. What *is* it about these books that leads so many of us to delve so deeply into them and then come up smiling with a wriggling inconsistency in one hand and a protesting, elusive error of fact only barely in the other? We are quick enough to drop our slippery handfuls and rush to the nearest bookshop on the day a new title is published. Bond and Fleming are laughed at and sneered at—they are pulled to pieces on all sides and from all angles. But they have never been rejected yet by the public.

'Fleming annoys me when he tries to get scientific,' I am informed by a friend with considerable technical knowledge. 'For instance, Bond's hotel room is bugged with a concealed microphone. Up the chimney is "a very powerful radio pick-up." What the hell has *radio* got to do with it?'

Similarly, 'Fleming gives the impression that he knows about guns. Yet Bond uses a Sniperscope, with an infra-red lens. He *sees colours* through it!' I checked this: actually one assumes that he does, but during the passage in question it is never definitely stated that either Bond or his companion see colours *through* that lens.

Again, I am observed reading *Moonraker* by a total stranger at a pub buffet. 'So you read Fleming, too? Good yarn, that. But have you ever tried working out the speed that submarine was travelling at to be anywhere near the spot that the rocket fell?' My book was open. Its title was not printed at the top of the page: neither verso nor recto. I submit that very few Bond addicts are able to identify a complete stranger's current reading from sidelong glances. Fewer still—only the rabid—in this particular bistro for barristers and the bowler-hat-brigade, would accost someone they did not know.

A professional spy of my acquaintance informs me earnestly that these books are 'all rot', and that activity in the Secret Service is not a bit as Fleming describes it. I didn't need this assurance: I never believed it was. But I know which—the real or the imaginative—makes the better reading.

These are all quibblings and criticisms made to me by others. I don't doubt that there are dozens more I have never heard. Attempting to pick holes in these books is becoming a national pastime: one rivalled, perhaps, only by nautical readers of C. S. Forester attempting to fault that author over technical details in the Hornblower books.* I have my own little conceits and conclusions re Fleming. Indulgence in them is one of the reasons I buy him: others have *theirs*, so *they* buy. This attitude of ours is one of the more intangible factors that go to make the best-seller. Fleming can't be unconscious of it: I believe he encourages it. After all, selling the books is the main object of the exercise.

I notice that he is very adept at picking up all sorts of odd little items of information and somehow letting them drop into the narratives casually, either through the words or the actions of his characters. Sometimes this irritates me: I think I know a lot more about the specific subject than he does. More often I find his habit endears me to him, particularly when I think I am able to recognize the source of his information: it makes me feel frightfully clever. I recall one example of this habit of Flemings' above all others. Some time shortly before *Goldfinger* was published, he and Raymond Chandler recorded a fascinating conversation for the B.B.C., which was heard on sound radio. It didn't get the publicity in those days that a similar programme might receive now, and I don't think that there are a great many people who remember it in detail. I was more fortunate in that somebody I knew went to the trouble of taping this duologue, and I had the opportunity of listening to it over and over. The conversation was saved from the banalities of a mutual admiration society by Fleming taking the ball and adroitly keeping it in play: Chandler did not seem too happy with the medium and had to be drawn out. But there was one passage I particularly remember, when he was talking about hoodlums and violence. 'When you're hit over the head and knocked out,' he said, or words to this effect, 'the first thing you do when you come to is vomit.' I don't *know* if Ian Fleming consciously stored away this piece of information in one of the pigeon-holes of his mind or if he absorbed it unconsciously, but it is a fact that in the very next book he wrote James Bond got knocked over the head and vomited

* I understand that nobody has done so yet.

immediately upon waking up. This *could* be coincidence, but a similar thing happens in a later book. Now there are plenty of coshings in the volumes pre-dating the Chandler conversation, but I have never noticed anyone throwing up in those under the same sort of circumstances.

Again, a few of the mysteries of Karate were popularized in the late 'fifties. It had quite a vogue. All is grist to the mill: *vide* Oddjob. Then, take Bond's assignment in *Diamonds are Forever,* and the big-business American gangsters: much of the local colour obviously derived from Kefauver. And remember that aeroplane incident in 1957, when a window broke and an unfortunate traveller was sucked out of the pressurized cabin over Persia? Possibly not, but it sticks in my own mind since I read about it in a newspaper *while travelling in a plane,* and I did not breathe easily until we had landed. Fleming also used this occasion to advantage, but I should add that he acknowledged his source in a Bond soliloquy.

On the irritation side, I am unusually interested in a somewhat off-beat story called 'The Property of a Lady', at the time of writing not available between the covers of a book, and only to be found—as far as I am aware—in the pages of an expensive but necessarily transient magazine.* Much of the action takes place in the auction room, the sort of locale with which I happen to be particularly familiar. The story carries a lot of the hackneyed lore and stereotyped drama of the sale room still accepted since things like Galsworthy's *The Skin Game* and Dornford Yates' tales—or probably before. 'I've never been to an auction before,' comments Bond. He is disappointed by the absence of all he had expected: the 'going, going, gone' rigmarole, for instance. Fleming, on the other hand, would appear to be considerably more familiar with auction room procedure, and putting Peter Wilson himself on the rostrum is a nice touch of local colour. But, speaking as one who has officiated at hundreds of auctions from the vantage-point of the desk beside the rostrum, my knowledge and experience make me wonder if Fleming doesn't know only very little more of what goes on than James Bond. Who on earth told him that it was considered bad form to turn round and see who was bidding against you? It's done all the time. And that gambit about the bidder having a secret arrangement with the auctioneer, who is to accept his bids as long as he keeps his glasses on— it's as corny as that other near myth (and I'm not lisping): 'Do you know, I once went into an auction room, and I

* *Playboy,* January, 1964

nodded my head to something my neighbour was saying, and *would* you believe it—the lot was knocked down to me!' As I say, I chafe at this sort of thing in Fleming's writing, but I don't stop reading him. I'd be sorer than ever if I did and then discovered, for example, that he had forgotten more about sales by auction than I had ever learned. This could well be so.

One could continue indefinitely in this strain, citing one's own observations or those that are brought to the attention by other addicts. I know one man who *fumes* at Fleming's dexterity—and temerity—in handling technical subjects he himself feels sure the author really knows little about, and at his own inability to put his finger on any actual error of fact in the text. 'Utter tripe,' says one of Fleming's fellow-authors, but I notice his familiarity with all the books. 'I hate him,' comments a very well-known publisher, tongue in cheek. 'I wish he was on *my* list.' Says the critic: 'Sex, sadism and snobbery.' Surely this is the best review Fleming ever had?

The fascinating thing about it all is that Bond and Fleming should provoke this sort of discussion. Very few people say to me: 'Can't read the stuff.'

I am reminded of a small party I attended in November, 1963. The conversation devolved upon the films of Alfred Hitchcock. After much representing and misrepresenting, *North by Northwest* was eventually reached. Inevitably, that amazing episode on the still, quiet and lonely road through the cornfields was recalled. Someone mentioned the helicopter. I said it wasn't a helicopter: just an ordinary plane spraying crops. But the damage was done. Helicopters in November meant the film of *From Russia, With Love*, the month before. Hitchcock was dropped and Fleming was picked up. Were we really to believe that a low-flying helicopter, equipped as it was, could fail to account for a solitary man in open country? I protested that this had nothing to do with Ian Fleming. *He* didn't write the film script. I thoroughly enjoyed the ensuing argument: it waxed and waned on the various merits and demerits of the books.* I recall few of the details now, but one remark remains in my memory. Of Dr. No's demise I shall never forget the awe and admiration in one voice as it rendered this judgment: 'What a wonderful way to kill a character—buried under a load of bird-shit!'

Other authors than Fleming have created people we read about from book to book. Many of them have grown

* Of seven people present, only one had never read the books. But even he had seen the films.

familiar. With the obvious exception of Sherlock Holmes, however, whom everybody knows about, very few of them could be brought into a conversation under almost any circumstances with the complete assurance that anyone present would understand the allusion. Between the wars, a mention of, say, Bulldog Drummond, Fu Manchu or Tarzan would give most listeners the gist of what you were talking about, even as Dr. Crippen's or Jack the Ripper's names today will set a very faint bell tinkling even in most 'teen-age ears. Thanks to the panacea of television, Ellery Queen and Philip Marlowe were talking-points a few years ago, among non-readers. Simon Templar and Inspector Maigret are household names today. Oh, by the way, ever heard of anyone named Perry Mason? (*Mere* names to me, like The Toff, Mike Hammer or—and I bow my head in shame—Hercule Poirot, might easily replace the others in a year or two.)

The point I am longwindedly trying to make is that mention of one James Bond is understood now in 1964 by practically everyone you might encounter. This, mark you well, entirely without a weekly series on the domestic screen. And no conflict, in this case, with 'The Play of the Week' or 'Sunday Night at the London Palladium'. The name is accepted by those who don't watch television, don't go to the cinema and don't read books. And there are such people, I assure you. I know one or two.

All literate beings, on this sceptred isle, with the possible exception of bedridden unfortunates quite incapable of observing current happenings, do their best to keep abreast of current events. Hospitalized patients, just able to raise a daily newspaper for a brief perusal, whether they read through to the current book and film news or whether they confine themselves to front-page items like the Kennedy assassination, High Court actions or 'Cathy Gale's' new contract, cannot avoid reading about James Bond.

The more fortunate of us, during the normal daily round, are assailed on all sides. Railway station bookstalls bludgeon us with his name. Posters on the Underground tell us 'James Bond is Back'. Newspapers carry interviews with his creator. Radio and television programmes continually evoke those magic words. Cinemas project his image. Pop-singers blare forth that saccharine theme-sone: 'Frummm Rushuh with Luuuuv . . .' I telephone the most insular of my acquaintances, and during our conversation I let drop the name: the allusion is immediately understood.

The man overwhelms me from all sides. Sated to the teeth with him and attempting, at the same time, to write about him. I confess I am hardly myself. Dealing with one of his exploits which involves sums of money of astronomical proportions, my table lamp catches part of the watermark as I roll a fresh sheet of paper into my typewriter.

64 MILL

What's this? Must be light-headed or something. I'm overworked. I roll the paper out again.

I should have known better. But I hold the sheet up to the light and read the rest of the watermark. Sure enough, there it is, in block capitals:

BOND EXTRA STRONG

SIGNET Mysteries You'll Enjoy

CALL FOR THE DEAD *by John Le Carré*
A canny British secret agent copes with an unusual case of espionage and murder. By the author of the big bestseller, *The Spy Who Came in from the Cold*.
(#D2495—50¢)

A MURDER OF QUALITY *by John Le Carré*
George Smiley, ex-espionage agent, exposes the deadly hypocrisy of England's oldest and finest public school as he uncovers a shocking and brutal murder.
(#D2529—50¢)

NERVE *by Dick Francis*
Unexplained suicides baffle the steeplechase set in this thunderingly vital suspense novel set in England.
(#P2607—60¢)

PURSUIT (The Chase) *by Richard Unekis*
A canny police superintendent matches wits against two desperate fugitives who have committed what looks like the "perfect crime." (#D2466—50¢)

INSPECTOR MAIGRET AND THE KILLERS
by Georges Simenon
Montmartre becomes the battleground for transatlantic gang war. (#D2579—50¢)

INSPECTOR MAIGRET AND THE STRANGLED STRIPPER
by Georges Simenon
Maigret in the Paris underworld of prostitutes, addicts, and killers. (#D2580—50¢)

INSPECTOR MAIGRET IN NEW YORK'S UNDERWORLD
by Georges Simenon
Breathless pursuit from plush Fifth Avenue to the slums of the Bronx. (#D2578—50¢)

TO OUR READERS: If your dealer does not have the SIGNET and MENTOR books you want, you may order them by mail enclosing the list price plus 10¢ a copy to cover mailing. If you would like our free catalog, please request it by postcard. The New American Library of World Literature, Inc., P. O. Box 2310, Grand Central Station, New York, N. Y., 10017.

GREAT ADVENTURES IN READING

THE MONA INTERCEPT 14374 $2.75
by Donald Hamilton
A story of the fight for power, life, and love on the treacherous seas.

JEMMA 14375 $2.75
by Beverly Byrne
A glittering Cinderella story set against the background of Lincoln's America, Victoria's England, and Napolean's France.

DEATH FIRES 14376 $1.95
by Ron Faust
The questions of art and life become a matter of life and death on a desolate stretch of the Mexican coast.

PAWN OF THE OMPHALOS 14377 $1.95
by E. C. Tubb
A lone man agrees to gamble his life to obtain the scientific data that might save a planet from destruction.

DADDY'S LITTLE HELPERS 14384 $1.50
by Bil Keane
More laughs with The Family Circus crew.

Buy them at your local bookstore or use this handy coupon for ordering.

COLUMBIA BOOK SERVICE (a CBS Publications Co.)
32275 Mally Road, P.O. Box FB, Madison Heights, MI 48071

Please send me the books I have checked above. Orders for less than 5 books must include 75¢ for the first book and 25¢ for each additional book to cover postage and handling. Orders for 5 books or more postage is FREE. Send check or money order only.

Cost $ _____ Name _____
Sales tax* _____ Address _____
Postage _____ City _____
Total $ _____ State _____ Zip _____

* *The government requires us to collect sales tax in all states except AK, DE, MT, NH and OR.*

This offer expires 1 September 81

8106

NEW FROM POPULAR LIBRARY

HAWKS 04620 $2.95
by Joseph Amiel

LOVE IS JUST A WORD 04622 $2.95
by Johannes Mario Simmel

NIGHT THINGS 04624 $2.25
by Thomas F. Monteleone

THE FOURTH WALL 04625 $2.25
by Barbara Paul

SCIENCE FICTION ORIGINS 04626 $2.25
Edited by William F. Nolan,
and Martin H. Greenberg

SAGA OF THE PHENWICK WOMEN #34,
URSALA THE PROUD 04627 $1.95
by Katheryn Kimbrough

Buy them at your local bookstore or use this handy coupon for ordering.

COLUMBIA BOOK SERVICE (a CBS Publications Co.)
32275 Mally Road, P.O. Box FB, Madison Heights, MI 48071

Please send me the books I have checked above. Orders for less than
5 books must include 75¢ for the first book and 25¢ for each additional book to cover postage and handling. Orders for 5 books or
more postage is FREE. Send check or money order only.

Cost $ _____   Name _____
Sales tax* _____   Address _____
Postage _____   City _____
Total $ _____   State _____ Zip _____

* The government requires us to collect sales tax in all states except
AK, DE, MT, NH and OR.

This offer expires 1 September 81   8098